WALG

WALG

A NOVEL OF AUSTRALIA

B. WONGAR

DODD, MEAD & COMPANY

NEW YORK

Published by Dodd, Mead & Company, Inc.
79 Madison Avenue, New York, N.Y. 10016

Distributed in Canada by
McClelland and Stewart Limited, Toronto

Manufactured in the United States of America

Designed by Helen Winfield

FIRST EDITION

Library of Congress Cataloging in Publication Data

Wongar, B.
Walg.

1. Australian aborigines—Fiction.   I. Title.
PR9619.3.W62W3   1983   823   83-11610
ISBN 0-396-08189-4

TO DJUMALA

*You shall be born again
as a bird, a tree, or a star,
as the tribal elders taught us.*

Sacred young girls of the northern tribes,
the evening sky smeared with menstrual flow
—the blood from a speared kangaroo,
from *walg*, the sacred uterus.
                —Fertility chant from Arnhem Land

This book is fiction; however, prior to the arrival of the white man some 550 tribes and 600 languages existed in Australia—only a handful of which survived.

According to the fertility cult of the Australian aborigines, the land is an extension of man's body and soul. This unity with nature ensures the regeneration cycles, and if the same be disturbed, life would consequently cease.

GLOSSARY

baba: father
babaru: large family, clan
baba-mugul: father's sister
badi: dilly bag, basket
bala: initiated
balanda: white man
bangduman: open legs, lovemaking position
banumbir: morning star, mes-
  senger from the spirit world
barbal: post, stilts
barlait: club
bilma: clapping sticks
birgurda: bees
boberne: mosquito
boong: derogatory term for
  aborigines
Bralgu: mythological island,
  land of the dead
bugalili: ritual invocation meaning revive, come to life again
burubu: hut
dagu: vulva, "woman's shade" on
  ceremonial ground
dagu win: long vagina, swear
dal: magic power, curse

dalhu: native grass
dalwadbu: turtle
darbal: frocked post
didjeridu: immense, deep-noted
  wind instrument made from
  hollow tree up to eight feet
  long
diridiri: pubic hair, growth
djabari: scorpion
djanda: goanna
djumala: whistling tree
  (casuarina)
djungawar: a sacred ceremony
djuwei: spirit, child's spiritual
  genitor
dua: one of two tribal moiety,
  maternal country
dudji: pair of fire-making sticks
dugar: track
dugaruru: stone, ritual emblem
duwei: man, husband
galamba: headband, armband
galdj: stone axe
galei: wife, woman
ganala: trench on ritual ground
  symbolizing a river

galnamiri: skin or body
ganinjari: digging stick
gara: spearhead, stone blade
garga: penis
gargman: frog
garuwuli: spider
"go-pass": compass
gulan: blood
gurung: male partner in ritual defloration of girls, cousin
gururgu: brolga
ingabunga: hole, ditch
jangulg: mainland
jarban: native bee, honey
jiridja: one of two tribal moiety, paternal country
kunapipi: fertility cult
larban: spear
lindarid: cockatoo, parakeet
mada: linguistic unit, "tongue"
maidja: breast girdle ("harness") worn by girls
mala: clan, group, people
malgu: flying fox
malnar: red ocher
malngud: two arms, dual
marain: totem, sacred, beautiful
marin: cabbage palm
marngit: medicine man, healer
maularin: labia majora
mauwulan: walking stick
mirigin: breast
miringu: revenge, manhunt
mogwoi: trickster spirit
momo: father's mother

mugul: cousin, niece
munji: wild berries
murlg: shelter, hut
muwuga: yams
nail: camp
nara: ceremonial festivities, foliage, hair
ngadu: damper made of cycad nut and used as ceremonial food
ngambi: stone blade used ritually
ngurubilga: wrong, improper
nigirnigir: cicada
njuga: mangrove crabs
nongaru: ceremonial ground for initiation of girls
ragia: bullrush
ranga: sacred ceremonial object
urban: emu
wadu: child
walg: womb, uterus, navel cord
wanba: wild pigeon
waragan: insects, birds and animals—all living creatures except humans
warngi: whale, sea monster
wawa: brother
wirgul: girl, daughter
wogal-dua: play story
wongar: beginning of the world, spirit world
wuramu: mortuary poles
wurulu: blowfly
yudu: semen
yuln: man

PREFACE

Some years ago I spent several days trapped in a paddy van, and my survival depended solely on the virtues of tribal poetry. I was caught in the Arnhem Land reserve, living on Crown land without the consent of government authorities, and was to be taken and jailed in the nearest settlement. I shared the paddy van with Jo Geleri; we were locked inside a cagelike box mounted in the back of a Land Rover with no canopy above, and as it was made of tough steel bars it gave little hope of escape. We were traveling along a bush track when the car broke down and the policeman left in a huff. Some hours later, we realized that we had been abandoned hundreds of kilometers from nowhere. "We'll get through," Jo tried to reassure me. It was September, the middle of the Dry, and the midday sun brought the air almost to boiling point. I was told to rest motionlessly, to position my body away from the sun and breathe through my nose.

As the sun's heat and glare declined toward the end of the day Jo began to mumble the verses of some old chant, trying to open his mouth as little as possible. It surprised me that he knew tribal poetry. He did not remember his father, a Rembaranga man, and his mother had brought him up at Delisaville camp, where the aborigines were grouped from various tribal areas and had to communicate among themselves in English.

His chanting was obviously related to a plea for rain, for we both knew that a man trapped in the sun without water would not last for even a day. "Some of the old tribal fellows must have taught you to sing?" I remarked later that day. "No, the song just came to my mind," he replied. He told me that he had never sung it before but had felt that the chant might be inside him. The following morning he sang again, and I accompanied him by tapping my fingernails against the chassis of the Land Rover. We remained motionless as the day grew hot again, and our strength had begun to fade when, in the afternoon, distant thunder sounded. A fresh breeze brought us back to life in time to see clouds banking up; they soon brought a downpour seldom seen at that time of the year. We were rescued the following day, but that would have been too late if the rain had not come.

For much of my understanding of tribal poetry, I am indebted to my late tribal wife, Djumala, through whom I was able to learn about the wide application of oral verses. In the reserve and the nearby area we lived from the bush as most of the economically independent tribal groups did at that time. The poetry was very much alive then; it was there, as so many generations ago, in order to show man how to live with his land and from the land.

I liked watching Djumala make the campfire; she never missed saying a few lines of verse to her two wooden sticks when she whirled one into the other (the smoke would often appear before all the words of the charm song had been uttered). There was one particular species of bush tree with pith inside the stem from which she made her fire sticks. Whenever she passed it in the bush she would say a few verses as though greeting a friend.

I once set a pile of wood on the fire, and raging flames burned the leaves from nearby trees. She told me a mythical tale of the emu woman who, taken by her husband to live with his tribe, felt afraid of the unknown country and made a big fire that caught the bush around and burned both her wings. Some days later I heard her in a camp singing with the other women what sounded like a contemporary song about a fire seen far away:

> On the backbone of smoke rides a stranger,
> Stony face shielded by flame
> In the bush each tree holds a spear.
>   Trees, be on the lookout
>   Poor fellow trees
>   Your bones are to turn into ashes.

In aboriginal poetry, the trees, as everything else, have souls. Some of them were tribal people reborn. Djumala used to hear them whispering at night. She convinced me that trees talk among themselves, that they often sing with their leaves and she could always tell by their voices whether they were male or female.

She knew of the ironwood tree under which the whites place their dingo traps. It always whispered to the animals to keep away whenever they appeared from the bush.

We once saw a cleared area of the bush with a long line of windgroves stretching across bare country and set ablaze. That night she woke me: "I just saw the trees fleeing the country. Now that the gums have learned to walk, the whites'll never get them." Some days later, looking at the Milky Way, she told me: "It's a trail of ashes across the sky left from the long windgrove." I reminded her that some tribal elders think it is a trail of the bones of the dead, then she added quickly: "Of course it is, the trees are our fellows."

When our first child was born, a stringybark gum in front of our rock shelter swayed and clapped one branch against another—a message sent away to tell other trees and the spirit world. She called the child Djo, Stringybark, and that same tree became his personal totem. I felt sorry that my ears were unaccustomed to the trees' songs, but I joined in and did my best to show respect to all gums, as one would do to his relatives. I avoided stripping the bark from tree trunks, and when I made a campfire I always took care that the branches should be far from the reach of the flames.

Djumala thought my kindness paid off. Once while we slept by the campfire on a river bank, a huge gum fell down during a night gale. We found ourselves suddenly between the fork of two large limbs that had crashed to the ground; had the tree swung a space the other way it would have crushed us.

I had to leave the area, not knowing how long it would be before I saw her again. I too, at this time, believed in the poetry and felt that however long my absence might be, the trees would care for her and the children. "You lean one ear against the trunk and listen to all that these fellows whisper," she often told me. The tree, like a faithful dog, wags its tail at you, I was made to believe, and that helped me to understand that we might meet again, as plants or birds.

Now and then I see trees in my dreams, fleeing from one district to another. They walk much slower than humans and often hold each other's hands. Behind them a herd of bulldozers is advancing fast, crushing the trunks and sweeping entangled branches into windgroves to set them ablaze. Djumala comes in my dreams to tell of a paperbark tree near a water hole that, dizzied by the sun, fell to warn her that the dingo trappers had been around and had poisoned the place. I doubt that she blames the tree but is perhaps trying to tell me to stay away from that water hole.

Walg was inspired by her.

B. Wongar

WALG

The Centre for Human Development
Camp Balanda, N.T.
5th October, 1980

My Dear Roger,

I had been hoping to visit the reserve again and stay with you for a while, but now that I have been honored with the most precious gift I must stay here and see that my dream comes true.

The facilities your corporation so generously gave us have far outreached my expectations. As you see from the photograph taken by that enthusiastic assistant of mine, Wuluru (or Butterfly as she prefers to be called), the metal structure looks gigantic and the photograph, of course, portrays only a portion of it. The enclosed compound will provide us with ample space to display the tribal festivities and though the fertility rites are, as you know, rather spectacular thanks to you, and to Adder's generosity, we will be able to set them in an air of traditional exactitude. I doubt that even old Gunbuna and my other tribal friends would notice that the setting is artificial.

Talking about Gunbuna, how is his tribal flock there? The experience of entering into this Atomic Age has been dramatic for many of us and how much more so for those Stone Age bush men ignorant of even a billy can.

Wuluru has convinced me that through living in his primitive state, aboriginal man has retained unique characteristics which, if properly utilized, could benefit all mankind. I will not bother you with biological theories, but Wuluru has a fine academic record in this field and has been fortunate to earn the trust of the aborigines by working among them as a nurse.

God bless you, my son.

Your affectionate father

1

The Centre for Human Development
Camp Balanda, N.T.
7th May, 1981
My Dear Roger,

We were nearly ready to begin our genetic program when the first setback struck; we lost our leading lady.

Thanks to Wuluru we found another woman, much younger and of good health, so thank heaven for that. She is a Galwan girl, but, unfortunately, I am unable to locate her amongst my genealogical data. Gunbuna, whom I had expected to tell me about her and of other bush lore has not only cut himself off from us and hardly communicates but has inspired other aborigines to follow suit. If you should come in contact with Gunbuna's brother, that wise medicine man, please be courteous to him, for though they are so many hundreds of miles apart, he can still exercise the power of his mind over these fellows here. Such things seem to work quite miraculously for them, as you know.

Wuluru has pointed out that our program would have come to fruition much more quickly had we established the center in the reserve. I cannot think of a better place than Durana Island, which you probably can see through your office window. Is the island, too, leased by the corporation from the Crown?

I hope to see you soon whether here or in the beloved bush.

May God bless you.

Your affectionate father

PART
ONE

CHAPTER ONE

During the night my mother called to see me. "I'll be off to our country," she whispered. She had on a pair of armbands made of cockatoo feathers and a newly woven string girdle that the girls wear on the day of initiation. She looked just like any one of us when we were brought down to *nongaru*, the "ceremonial ground." "We all have to go through this sooner or later." Her voice sounded excited but shy, as it would have done on the day they made her into a woman.

I'd better get up, look for some more wood and see to the camp fire. The night has been cold, and though the sun will show soon, the chill still lingers in the air. Yes, mother sat for a while there on the log, staring at the ashes and gathering the coals together with her *ganinjari* ("digging stick") trying to make the flames flare up. I thought she was going to lie down to rest and I moved to make room for her; Muru, my dog, got up and left a warm place behind me; the ground is dusty out here but warm. She moved closer and loomed over me, curled up in the sandpit. "Shouldn't you have a child? Every black woman bears some; you've made the shelter."

5

There are two rusty corrugated iron sheets lying sideways to form a fork shape; they do not make much of a shelter, but they keep the night winds away. One of the sheets has several holes in it, and when the gusts come they whistle through them for hours and conjure up the sight of everyone you know; you can hear a whole tribe whispering to you that way. My cousins from the bush often come to chat with me; all of them—*jiridja* and *dua*—"father's and mother's side of the family." Now and then I hear Bungul, a man I was betrothed to, calling through that rusty iron, too. He is still angry but less hurt and should come to realize that whatever one does or is forced to suffer, sooner or later we shall all meet in Bralgu, our spirit world.

I should be careful with fire. If it is allowed to smoke heavily, it might chase the spirits away, and mother might still be hanging around the camp. Her skin, darker than mine, looked heavily smeared with red ocher and kangaroo fat; it cast the fresh, earthy smell of the ceremonial color. Beautiful, she looked again, twisting her breast girdles. The sound of clapping sticks and *didjeridu*, our pipe, rose in the air, followed by a chant heard only on the initiation ground.

Daybreak feels much cooler than the night; I have to strike half a burned log to loosen a few clumps of glow and some sparks; twigs and dry leaves will catch fast. I shall throw a piece or two of wood over them and let that burn slowly. "You don't need a big fire for a single soul." Had mother told me that in my dream during the night or had I heard it days ago? She had held a small oval stone while she loomed over me. The stone looked the same color as her skin, rubbed with red ocher and sacred. It is called *dugaruru*. Up in the bush in the old days the women used to carry these stones around and pound palm nuts on them . . . they may be used for something else as well. The elders say the stone has some power, perhaps to do with birth; each woman has to have one of her own if she is to bear children. In Galwan, my country, they seldom talk about *dugaruru*, which is only seen once a year when the tribe gathers for the big *nara*, the ceremony during which the stone appears from some hidden place and cycad palm nuts are pounded on it for the men. When the festivity is over, it disappears until the next gathering. I have not seen the stone for years now, and I have forgotten the little I knew about it. Perhaps I should ask Wagudi; the old man has a fire behind the bushes up at the far end of the camp, and he will tell me something of what a woman of my age should know.

Muru is up, too; he usually sleeps until the sun is spear high, but now he sniffs around even though it is only daybreak. His head rises toward the clumps of bamboo with his nostrils soaking up the air and and he squeals, glancing at me as though there is something I should do. Down near the river there are some bushes, not far, only a whistle away. Perhaps later on I should go and look around. Mother could be hiding there in the bushes, too scared to come out and be seen around the camp. The tribal people are shy and easily frightened.

Look, *dugaruru* is here, resting on the top of a log. Mother wanted me to have it. The stone must have been in use for a very long time; its surface has been smoothed by the hands that worked it, and a small hollow in the middle shows where the nuts were crushed once a year, but . . . who can count how many years it has been in use. The Galwan people say that when the first black woman came to give birth, the stone came out of her womb and has been used ever since.

The sun is about to rise; it has already lit up the treetops. I'd better hide *dugaruru*; the whites could be around soon. A road skirts the camp, passing along the long embankment and over a bridge across the ravine; it heads toward town, farther away. From up there you can see even a single footprint in the dusty ground. Whenever they are about, the whites like to stand on the embankment and stare down here. Wagudi thinks the *balandas* are counting how many of us are left. I have to go later and see Wagudi; the elder might tell me if mother is still about. He might chant and sound his *didjeridu* to beg her to visit us again; the spirits can easily be persuaded to come if you only know the right way.

That ceremonial chant still lingers about:

They think of the boomerang with flattened point
Pushing her down, that girl on the man's hip, into the branches.

The whites would not know about our dreams, but the news must have got about that mother had been to see me. The welfare nurse, *wurulu* the blowfly, we call her, roars into the camp in her car, faster than ever before, trailing behind an immense serpent of dust. "We almost forgot about you, Julia." The nurse steps carefully, plunging her white shoes into the dust. She used to call in often, long ago, when there were more camp fires alight, to bring a blanket or two, or bundles of half-worn clothes. She often hung around, staring at everyone to see whose skin suffered from rashes or sores so that she could take him away and heal it. The elders did not like it and called her *wurulu*, the blowfly that hangs around and sucks your soul out when it smells blood on the skin.

"Here. Have some barley sugar and a box of matches. You mustn't let your fire go out."

Wherever she goes Wurulu wears a smile, but our people think she brings more harm than good. Wagudi worries the most. Whenever the nurse's car is seen rolling down from the road he is like a shooting star, rushing off to the river and dashing behind the bushes to keep away until she has gone.

"One of our ladies has got loose; have you seen her?"

8

Someone must have watched me from the embankment holding *dugaruru* stone or noticed that mother was here. Our spirits are not always discreet; they call in when they feel like it. Lucky she came during the night; had she called in the daytime half the town would have flocked across the river and stared from the embankment to watch the ceremony of her initiation.

"But she ought to be somewhere," said Wurulu.

"I'm the only woman left in the camp. Most of our people have gone."

"This one was much older than you, but Doctor Cross hoped she might still produce. He provided her with a cozy place to encourage her to bear."

The nurse took a photograph from her bag that showed a large enclosure looking like an enormous cage. Instead of a door, the structure had a funnellike passage to lead the newcomer deep inside, and hanging on the wall, just below the entrance, was a larger plaque. I don't read the white man's lingo, but there is a word—ADDER—and something else written on it.

"It's quite an innovative dwelling, donated to us by a mining corporation; it could accommodate a whole tribe. If there were enough of you inside, you could hold your festivities, just like in the good old days."

She must be thinking of our fertility ceremony, *nara*; the whites would like to watch us dancing naked and making ritual love. Some time ago news spread in the town that we were to hold *nara* at the camp here. *Balandas*, the whites flocked to the embankment, buses brought tourists, some coming from half a world away with their cameras and binoculars, and they saw nothing but the campfires here.

The nurse moves the photograph closer, tilts it away from the blinding sun and then points her finger at the funnellike passage: "See, at the end of the entrance, here, one falls inside. . . . It's high up, but there is a pool on the ground below. You

9

splash like you do in a billabong when you go for the ritual bath with the men up in the bush."

The enclosure reminded me of a huge trap: "How do you get out of there?"

"Why leave? Everything is inside. We're going to organize that fertility ceremony for the inmates. You call it *nara*; all the tribe gathers in a billabong for a communal bath and then they mate ritually." She stayed silent for a moment, gazing at my body: "Doctor Cross is developing a new breeding program— family planning."

Wurulu walked around the fire the way one does when there is nothing else to say or do. She stepped on the edge of the ash mound where the stone *dugaruru* was hidden; the fire is the only place the whites do not poke their noses when they happen to be here.

"Julia, look around for that stray woman, would you. She could wreck the whole family planning project."

How is it that the *balanda* could never remember that my name is Djumala—it means whistling tree; Ranger and the others call it casuarina. One of them is growing in Galwan where I was born. Mother must have sat in the shade under it to have me. I hear my name rarely here; Wagudi, the elder, calls me *wirgul*, but I am never sure if he means "grandchild" or "tribal daughter." The others use the name of my clan totem— *lindarid*.

The nurse dashed to her car and then walked back: "Look what I have brought for your dog; is the animal still around?" Poor Muru, scared stiff, is hiding behind the corrugated sheets with only the top of his ears showing. Animals are like humans, they can tell when you are after them.

She calls him "Woolly," but there is nothing woolly about him; the dog has hardly any fur left. Something strange has happened to his hair; most of it has fallen out, leaving behind only red skin that reminds me of *gargman*, a "frog."

The nurse stares up at Muru. "It's mange; the poor beast needs treatment—I'd better take it away."

"No, he has to keep me warm. It's often a five-dog night here."

"You should have a man to keep you warm."

The camp is just about empty. There were only a few elderly people and even they found their way out of here, leaving behind a fire mound and an empty hole in the sand where they had rested. Wagudi is about the only one left, and his turn might be next. "The dog is one of us."

She tries hard to understand me, but her face hardens. "You sleep with them in a manner of speaking, she says. The people in the town see that differently."

"See what?"

"They do gossip, you know. Especially after what happened at that dreadful place . . . Gin Downs." She pronounced the last two words as though she were washing her mouth with them.

"I have never been to Gin Downs."

"Julia, that was some years ago. All those who were there . . . I doubt that any black girl got away from that place." The leaves on the bamboo clumps rustle suddenly; distracted, she glanced at the bushes down by the river. "What about the tribal elder Wagudi . . . hasn't he told you all about it?"

My *momo* ("grandmother") was there and had much to tell. The place apparently is near the Reserve border. From there the bands of whites used to raid our land to seize the tribal girls. I should keep quiet about *momo*; the less *balandas* know about your tribal relatives, the better. "Were you at Gin Downs?"

"No white women were there." She mellowed apologetically. "Don't bother with those stories; when in the bush, men's minds run wild. A smile shows again in the corner of Wuluru's

11

mouth: "Come to us at the center. Look, the town is just across the river. You know where to find us, the center is what used to be the old mission place. The young fellows will be there—Plonk, Dadangu and many others. The only woman we had has just vanished."

You do not just leave the campfire and the pit filled with clean river sand to rest on. Though it is only a hole in the ground, it is warm and as familiar as someone you have known for years. Every tree from here down to the river and high up to the road has its own voice and its own manner of swaying in the wind. The branches, a chatty lot, carry on and whistle to each other all night. Perhaps the trees also have their own songs and chants, but humans never sit still long enough to hear and learn their lingo.

"How long have you had the dog?"

"It's a dingo; it came a long way, from Galwan, my country."

"It looks pathetic, very like U . . . Uuuuu . . . that skin relative of yours."

Ure is the brother of Bungul, the brother of the man I am betrothed to. I don't like her talking about him. "Each dog carries the soul of one of your dead relatives; that is why the animal holds on to you."

"A friend of mine had a dingo; he never claimed it to be his brother though. Some of those witch doctors have twisted you around, all right."

Perhaps I said more than I should have; the *balandas* believe in nothing but what pleases them.

The nurse's face hardened. "That cur wouldn't even warm a flea."

"Muru is the only dog I have."

"It carries disease; if the sickness spreads, even humans will be affected and lose their hair. It happened at Gin Downs."

Across the river rushes a willy-willy; the wind hits the bushes

12

at the edge of the camp, rips off branches and sends them up in a whirlpool into the sky.

Wuluru moves closer. "We had a dreadful epidemic here some years ago," she said. "It almost wiped out all of you. Julia, haven't any of your fellows told you about it?"

"No." Why would our dogs bring us any harm? The whites are the ones we have to fear.

"Wagudi—that old man Ure hangs about with when he's here—he must remember the plague. Doctor Cross saved his life. The plague started at Gin Downs and spread across the whole reserve. It wiped out many of your tribes."

Who is she after?

"Were it not for old doc, none of you would be alive."

The bamboo groves sway, hit by the sudden gust; the stems hold onto the roots but the leaves, a whole swarm of them, float into the air. I see mother again, her limbs tumbling among the leaves.

When the air cleared, Wurulu was sitting in her car with Muru behind her clawing the window and whining to be let out.

"It has to be taken to the vet."

The nurse drove off before my voice could reach her. The line of dusty cloud serpented through the camp again, passed the row of dead fires, dodged the few remaining trees and ended on the edge of the highway.

CHAPTER TWO

Luckily there is someone here to call on; our tribal elders know all about *dugaruru* and anything else that is sacred. They would tell us about every tribal custom and never forget a chant. Wagudi does it better than any of them: "We will all go back to our country," he says often, leaving every black soul to wonder whether we will return to Galwan as humans or as spirits.

Not much shows from Wagudi's fire by day. The elder lets the fire blaze at night, and with the dawn the smoke subsides— all but a few scraps that might be seen lingering around the branches of the gum trees. He stays beyond reach of the camp, farther down where the sloping ground falls fast into the river ravine choked with thick vines and bushes—just the place to hide *dugaruru*. The stone has to be kept hidden away. With Muru the dog gone, the whites could creep into the camp and snatch it from me. "Without that treasure, no black man will be born," I was told in Galwan, our tribal country.

Should I tell Wagudi that Wuluru knows Ure has been here?

My mother might have called to see Wagudi too. He is my father's brother and head of our *babaru* ("clan"). The stone is sacred to all of us—no elder would let it be taken. I have brought *ganinjari* ("digging stick") with me—we might have to make a hole and bury the stone. The ground near the river will be hard to break; I have been down there many times searching for *muwaga* ("yams") through the bush. There are tree roots everywhere, but if you dodge them, several hard jabs in the ground should do the job. That *didjeridu* heard yesterday when mother appeared—it was he who played it. No other black man blows the pipe so ardently.

No smoke from the fire shows yet but the top of the trees under which Wagudi camps are seen now. Why stay away from the rest of us? I should ask the elder if he would like to move into the camp, and then I would not need to walk so far when I want to talk to him. There is a big tree hardly a spear's throw from my place. The branches are all dead and the wind is often caught in the partly peeled bark, howling so you can hear it half a camp away. Someone has lived there but left long ago; a corrugated iron sheet still leans against the tree trunk, and under it there is a Hessian bag stretched on the ground. Wagudi would like it; the old people prefer to have *murgl* ("shelter") over their heads, and then when there is a downpour they are not ill afterward.

It is a pity that mother did not say much when she came last night. There are no Galwan women ready to learn what to do with *dugaruru* and how you go about bearing a child. She might come back tonight. If not I'll have to go down to the river and search among the bushes; spirits like to linger by pools of water, and if you know the right words to say or chant, they'll come to you.

Smoke shows above the top branches of the gums. No, it is only the drift of dust left by a willy-willy. Wagudi will not like that; his eyes grow wet and itchy when the dust sweeps the camp. The elder rubs them and they run red. Trachoma, Wurulu calls it; the nurse has tried hard to make him go with her to the center to be cured. I doubt if he has ever been across the river; he might never go. How long since he left Galwan? He never says. But he knows about Plonk—much more than I do—and even calls him *yuln*, "tribal man." I often saw them sitting in the shade chatting for half the day. Some days ago I walked with Wagudi through the camp, counting the dead fires. He stood for a moment at each: "The soul is here, left behind in the ashes." That tempest blow of the *didjeridu* he played last night is the sound you hear at *nongaru* ("ceremonial ground") while the men make you into a woman; you live with it forever after.

No smoke can be seen rising from Wagudi's fire, but it is still a good voice to his place. I have never asked the elder how they brought him here—by sea or land. Coming from our country to here, you move from one world to another like flocks of flying foxes or birds do when they are driven by drought. Man has to make his way across the land. There is a track from Galwan to here, stretching through the reserve from one water hole to another, and whichever time of year one is forced to travel, you have to make more camps than any of the blacks could count. Yes, Wagudi must know what the country along that track looks like. Some days ago I watched him helping Ure to make a spear-thrower, heating a piece of plastic pipe to reshape it. "There won't be many trees left there to cut proper tools from," he said. "This stuff melts easily; keep it away from the fire whenever you camp." How would Wuluru know that Ure had been here?

Not one of our fellows was here when I first came, except Plonk perhaps, but soon afterward the camp was swollen by a flood of them. So many poor souls. It looked as though an angry river had swept through Galwan after a great storm and brought down with it every single tree you had grown up with or sheltered under. They floated down in a torrent—the men of our *babaru* and other tribal families. Many of them I know, the others I have seen in the bush now and then, or when they crowd down to the shore to hold *nara*, the longest of our ceremonies. Swept down here, too, are black men I have never seen but perhaps met in a dream or in a life before this one. I wonder how long the track back to Galwan would be. Even if it takes a year or two instead of a full moon, some of us would make it. I should ask Wagudi; he traveled that way—from one end of the reserve to the other—with old Gunbuna, Ure's father. Perhaps . . . yes, the elder will tell me all about it. Gunbuna, he too, was there last night; who else would have clapped *bilma* sticks to accompany the *didjeridu*. The two men played together the day I was initiated.

The trunk of the old gum tree Wagudi camps under can be seen now. Some smoke should be wisping up, lingering for a while round the tree before sneaking out from the branches to drift toward the sky and melt into the air. The elder might be asleep . . . no, I doubt if he would want to stay under that dead tree where someone lived before. Yesterday we had a long walk through the camp. "Each of those fires has a soul. The men might go but the spirits linger," he told me. When a man goes away from his country he has nothing to hold on to but the fire, and when he dies the spirit stays near it. The ashes of some fires are almost washed away, leaving behind nothing more than a gray patch and a handful of charcoal. Yet Wagudi would know who first lit it and could read from the fire the fellow's whole life. Would he talk to me about my mother?

I shall say nothing of that to Plonk and Dadangu. The elder might have been sent from our tribal country to watch over us all and when hard times come to chant some of those magic words to our spirits to come with help. I watched him long ago trying to help Plonk, although that youth is half white and born here. The elders do not mind what one's skin looks like as long

17

as the soul is ours. Yes, Plonk is from our *babaru* all right. He's a young man now, they might have to initiate him soon. Though far from Galwan we must stick to our customs—what else is there for the black man to cling to? Mother might have spoken to Wagudi about Plonk. How else would the elder know the lad is one of us?

The elder is nowhere to be seen. Maybe he has wandered down to the river to look for some food—tortoises perhaps; he likes them best. I have caught some for him before, but if he shifts closer to my fire I will go every day to get him one. Tortoises are not hard to find; they hide in pools along the river. I have a large container, given to me by Plonk, and though it has a few holes you can bucket out a small pool if you work fast enough. Even Wuluru knows how much Wagudi likes tortoise. She brought him a blanket the other day and a can of prawns. "We don't tin tortoises, but he might like to eat these," she said as she left the food. Then she added, "That old fellow Gunbuna used to be mad on prawns. Doctor Cross told me so."

The ground has begun to slope steeply; I have to hold onto the bushes so as not to slide down to the ravine. The *balandas* never walk to the river this way; it is a place of snakes and red spiders. There will be a few *djabari* ("scorpions") too, down there, creeping among the shady bushes. None of that would worry Wagudi. The white man's world across the river, that is what frightens him.

Across the bridge rattles a heavy truck. Leaving the earth trembling behind, it howls along the embankment toward the rubbish dump farther off into the bush. Yes, Wagudi must have gone down to the tip; there is a well-beaten track along the edge of the ravine. But even without that to follow, the smell will lead you there. No, something must have happened—Wagudi's fire is almost dead. A spark of red shows here and there in the ashes, but that too will fade away soon. Over the ashes lies a lizard,

18

burned into charcoal and long forgotten; it will be too tough for even a dog to eat.

Wagudi's *didjeridu* must be around here somewhere. He usually hides it in the bushes over there, but . . . he will be upset when he learns it is gone. I used to hear him playing the pipe every night; the sound rises not long after dusk with a deep roar that echoes through the gum branches before floating into the sky. When he is blowing *didjeridu*, the elder pokes the end of the pipe into a hollow tree and makes it roar louder. He hopes the sound will reach Galwan and travel even farther, across the sea to the land of our spirits. Why did they take him away? Someone must have dobbed him in for helping Ure with that spear. The whites do not like the sight of our tools; a spear must give them a gut reaction—"weapon" they call it.

High up on a thick branch rests a white bird; it is *lindarid*, cockatoo. It makes a sound but too faintly to tell whether it is a call or a squawk. One of the bird's wings hangs down with several feathers sticking out from the rest. The crest looks crooked too, leaning to one side of the head. The cockatoo tries to raise it, but the sulfur fan only springs half open. It must be that same bird I watched being tumbled by the willy-willy; it was lucky to escape. When you are tossed by the wind with so little to hold on to, you have to be more than a living soul. Only those with *dal*, "the magic power of the spirit," can find their way out. The bird tilts its head, watches me with one eye and tries to screech. It is not so much a cry as a chat to someone you know.

I wish the bird would tell me something about Wagudi and Ure: she should know all about us—we all come from the same flock.

CHAPTER THREE

The place where a man is born becomes his country, says a Galwan custom. Here that might not mean much. There are still vast tracts of bush around the town, but the whites will not give it to any of us even if you are only partly black and born here like Plonk. I doubt if he worries much about land. He lags several steps behind trying to say something but only mumbles. Words come out the hard way if your mouth is crippled. As soon as we cross the bridge I will slow down and have a chat. Why does he want me to go to town with him? He might know where the *balandas* have taken Wagudi and the other fellows. Even so, there will be a concrete wall or wire fence, for sure, to keep us off. Anyway, the elder is head of our *babaru* ("family"); it will be good to know where they are keeping him.

Plonk points to a cluster of towers beyond the scrub plain: "A-a-a-a-anthill." He too must wonder why the whites have to live like ants. It could not be for warmth. More likely the fear that our spirits might rise from the bush has forced them to hug together in the place they call town. Days ago, I heard Wagudi telling Plonk and Dadangu that the spirit of the blacks could be

20

disguised . . . as a tree or a bird. A stretch of cleared land rings the town, but on the other side of the river lies a whole forest. The trees look safe, for the whites cross the bridge only now and then, always riding in their cars, to snatch a soul or two from the camp. Whoever is taken away is not seen again, though he might come back—no longer as a human being—to be heard wailing in the branches of the tall trees. The voices often sound faint, no one but Wagudi can tell what the words mean; the elders, like *marngit*, our "medicine man," can talk to the spirits.

"Do you hear wailing at night, too?"

Plonk knocks his head with his hand instead of struggling with the words. One knock should mean "yes" and two "no." Or was it the other way around? His mouth has turned sideways, facing over his left shoulder, and the words can only get through after a long struggle. Before the curse struck, he used to chat, learned our lingo and could talk just as any of us born in Galwan. But now, with part of his face crippled, instead of the word *balanda* he often stutters "b-b-b-boss." He might have seen the whites taking Wagudi away during the day. Plonk hangs around our camp if he is not in the town, and at night he walks to the rubbish dump down the river and squeezes into a derelict water tanker to rest.

"Have you heard anything about Ure and Dadangu?" I asked. The men used to sleep with him in the tanker, but now both of them are gone.

Plonk lifts his hand and taps it against his forehead; the look on his spotty face and in his deep, light eyes says no. I used to watch Dadangu and him walking along the embankment from the rubbish dump, crossing the bridge and disappearing down the road to the town. "They should stick to the bush, like Ure!" Wagudi did not like to see Plonk leading the others across the river, not because his skin is lighter but because he is less

21

cautious of the whites.

It feels hot; the sun has turned the road into a bed of red-hot ashes. It is a pity that the trees have been stripped from the land, Plonk wants to rest in the shade. Streams of sweat roll down his forehead. There is a nasty mark on his face: it looks as if someone has slashed the spotty skin with a broken bottle. Did mother drink, too? No one says much, though she mixed with the whites more than any of us. Whether she boozed or not, Plonk must have grown up on it instead of milk.

"U-u-ure fled; *balanda* at the rubbish dump s-s-say." He struggles to smile.

"What else do they talk about there?"

"W-w-wagudi's been taken. We're all to be locked up soon."

Plonk could not have found a better place to camp than that dump. Most of the discarded bottles are empty, but whenever I was there to look for food, I used to see him, with Ure and Dadangu, tipping the flagons to see if there was any left. He will have to search on his own now. Yesterday he came to see me down in the camp; he had found a pair of shorts on the dump, like the ones that Ure used to wear. His voice gave up completely, leaving only sighs struggling through the crippled mouth. I tried to look calm, telling him that Ure must have run away from the jail and could be on the way back to Galwan. You do not need the white man's rags in our tribal country.

We are almost in town. The large compound ringed by walls and strands of wire through which is seen the top of a banyan tree is hardly a voice away now. Behind it rises a yellow building with more windows than any of us know how to count. They used to call the place the mission, long ago. Wurulu says it is a center now—a place where many of us are taken to learn not to trespass on the white man's land across the river. It is for our own good, she thinks: those inside the compound will learn to eat with a spoon and wear a cloth around their waists. Wagudi

22

does not believe her. "It's a jail," he says. And if any of us is kept there for long, his skin might change to white and no black *marngit* would be able to lift the spell.

"Would they let us see Wagudi?"

"N-n-no." Plonk grimaces toward the compound, passes the yellow building hurriedly and leads me to a square. Mother might be hiding in the town if she is still about; perhaps I am being taken to see her. No, I doubt if Plonk has ever been told that mother is here. Wagudi would say no word about it, and Ure and Dadangu would not either. Both of them are my age, and mother left Galwan before I learned to walk properly.

In a shop window in the square, a vast bush scene unfolds on the screen of a box. Thick paperbark forest conceals the land; whistling trees have broken through the green canopy here and there and, thriving upward, are silhouetted against the sky. Why does it look reddish?

"T-t-t-t-television. You'll see our *nara* place." Plonk's hand sweeps across the glass. Yes, the red color is the reflection of a large flame tree growing at the square.

The scene changes and the country now looks as though it is seen from a cloud floating above it. The sound of *didjeridu* and clapping sticks rises from somewhere and it, too, floats above the forest. Down there lies Djangau Peninsula, like a woven hat, fringed by the white rim of the rising tide. I have seen that shape of the country before, drawn on a paper, when I was traveling with Ranger. He called it "chart" and often took the paper from his rucksack to tell us which way to go—a crumpled sheet with torn pieces hanging from the edges and looking unlikely to hold together to the end of the trip. Now the country on the screen looks much different. Even Mount Wawalag is there, sitting on the far end of the peninsula with the twin cliffs of the sisters rising from the summit to tickle the soft belly of the clouds.

23

"G-g-g-Galwan."

The tribal boundaries were not shown on the chart, nor on the screen; however, one runs along the peninsula, dividing it into two halves. The western part belongs to Narku, and the eastern part is ours. How would Plonk know about the tribal country? He has never been there. Yes, it must have been her. From whom else would Plonk have come? I doubt that he has grown up with her. And even if he has, you do not learn much of the tribal customs and life in the bush if you live in the white man's world.

It is a lagoon, lying near the tip of the peninsula between the mountain and the sea. It looks pretty when it is seen from the Wawalag slopes, like an immense turtle coming out of the sea and nesting in the plain of the cycad palms. Each year the tribes gather there to hold *nara*, the life-increasing ceremony. I doubt that Plonk could have heard about the lagoon from Wagudi. The elder would not talk much about tribal festivities to an uninitiated youth. He might have learned something from Ure and Dadangu; they have both reached their manhood and would have gone through the ceremony had we been in the bush.

"Nowhere else has nature given us so much for so little." Ranger! He is on the screen, a small stone in his hand; his voice has mellowed to a smile. I have not seen Ranger since our journey from Galwan. He looks younger now; there is no longer a beard on his face and his bushy hair, which before looked like a clump of dry straw, has been combed and trimmed. The white man sneers. "Gunbuna, that good old chief, invited us here to flatten the country." Blood stains his face—no, it's that flame tree again.

Why didn't our men kill him?

"There are mountains of these precious stones here in the bush." Though Ranger's lips move, the words seem to come from a corner of the box instead of his mouth. He tilts the stone on his palm forward; instead of his other hand there will be only an empty sleeve, but he shields it. I wonder how the chest wound has healed; it cannot be seen behind the white shirt and tie. Years ago, it was . . . no, the chest wound was not so deep; I doubt that it was caused by a spear at all. More likely it was a cut he got by falling down on a rock or a stump while he was trying to run through the bush quicker with his head than his legs could follow. The arm—that was quite a mess. I put white cotton over the wound and wrapped it with the rags from his shirt, but the blood still found its way through and it clotted only when a few handfuls of dust were thrown over it.

"Nature here has enriched us with so much to enjoy." Ranger holds the rod of a Geiger counter, pointing it upward.

Beside me mumbles Plonk. How much would he know what had happened to our country?

The stone in the white hand moved closer to cover the whole screen. "A single stone like this can light your home for decades. It gives the power that you and I . . ." The stone looks like . . . *dugarudu!* It is the same shape as the one given to me by my mother. They are all gray, spotted here and there with *malnar*—red ocher that shows they are taken from inside the womb.

Plonk points to the screen again: "B-b-b-b . . ." It looked for a while as if he was trying to say "boss," but catching a breath he finally struggled out with "b-b-bastard!"

Something has happened to the picture box. The stone in the white hand trembles. Then the whole scene slides into darkness, and with it the reflection of flame tree fades away, too.

CHAPTER FOUR

The night went by without the dog or a fire, and it was not as hard as it looked at first. Luckily I found an old car at the rubbish dump to crawl into; although the springs showed through the worn seat cover, it was still good to stretch out on. I found two Hessian bags as well, slid into one and covered my shoulders with the other. There is no safer place to rest than the dump. Our fellows think the whites only come here during the day to dispose of their refuse and then, hounded by the stink, hurry back. The rats, bandicoots and dingoes struggle through the wrecks and piles of rubbish looking for food, but the animals are hounded just as we are.

Our fellows were around all night—Gunbuna, Wagudi, Ure, Dadangu, Plonk and many others from both Galwan and Narku clans. They sat in a circle, right there in the clearing where the blade of a bulldozer had scraped off the topsoil. At first I thought it was a ceremony to initiate our young men; some of the fellows held their spears and I felt uneasy. The women should not watch the gathering if it is *marain* ("sacred"), but they were only chatting, not chanting. With them sat Marngit

26

holding a boomerang and drawing lines with it on the ground while he looked at Ure.

"Go along the river—more camps than you have fingers and toes altogether." Marngit had a deep voice, but it sounded empty like the wind in the hollow trees. In Galwan he lived on Mount Wawalag, and whenever there was a gathering—for good or bad—he came down and, maybe because of his *dal* ("magic") and the way he knows not only the country but the spirits as well, he always had a lot to say. Not only Narku, *dua* people, but our *jiridja* fellows listened to him as well. "Watch out when you're at Gin Downs; there are many *ingabunas* around there.

"Old mining pits—the bush is littered with them," explains Gunbuna.

The boomerang moves. "*Wirgul*, our girls, will be there to shield you from the place."

When in Galwan, Marngit's hair was held back by *galamba*, "woven belt"; now he wears a strip of orange plastic around his head instead. Several strips of paper, blown off the dump, have caught in his hair, hanging loose ends down his forehead and tickling his eyes persistently. In the tribal country he kept his beard neatly; the gray hair firmly in place looked like a sea shell hanging down from the old face. My *momo* thought the beard of the healer had to be kept white, for whenever he is here to help and to chant "Bugalili," he has to be seen as well as heard by our spirits. "When you're hounded by the *balandas*, cling to the sooty boulders of the burned country—they're the color of our skin."

Marngit's beard looks different now; the hair has broken up into small clams showing between the patches of peeling skin. It looks like a handful of straws gummed with resin. The light color of the beard has changed to that of the earth and reminds me of a possum's tail rotting in a trap. No matter what Marngit's face gives away, his voice still sounds out well: "Once you get to the plateau go toward the sun when it is seen in the morning. There aren't many water holes there—the Milky Way track will lead you from one to another."

I heard Wagudi once chatting to our fellows about that track and . . . yes in Galwan, *momo* told me something about how she traveled along the Milky Way, too. It is not a track across the sky but some marks on the ground across the reserve.

"If you are stuck, call on us."

Ure looked at the boomerang drawing the line on the ground and hardly blinked. The old man is his *baba*, "father and a Narku elder." Something has happened to Ure's hair, too; it had almost all fallen out, leaving behind only a few patches that, on the inflamed red skin, reminded me of the stunted bushes on the dunes of the red sand. On the forehead above his left eye there was a hollow, as though someone had stamped hard with his heel on the soft soil of the ground. He is only a few years older than I. As children we used to play *wogal-dua* together, the story about Boma-Boma, a man from the Dreaming—our mythical past—who tried to seduce his cousin Ji. They lived in the time before woman learned about the *dugaruru* stone and could not bear children.

"Watch out for *balandas*, the whites have spread through the bush like flies, chipping the rocks and sniffing the soil. Don't let yourself be easily tracked—leave no marks behind, and bury the ashes of every campfire."

Ure was leaning on his spear. The grip of his fingers loosened suddenly and his hand slid down the shaft, leaving behind a wet mark.

Under the tip of the boomerang, the country unfolded as it did when last seen on the TV box. Of the trees, only the trunks remained and, stripped of branches and bark, looked like matchsticks scattered through a vast desert. The boomerang made its way between them and, harrowing a path through the dust, headed toward Djangau Peninsula shrunk under a stormy sky. "Be at Gururgu Crossing at early dawn to pass over safely. Traps are set during the day; hardly even a cockatoo gets through."

Not far from them, Plonk kept busy checking discarded flagons at the dump. In front of him rose an immense pile of empty bottles. He sipped a drop or two from some of them and crawled up the heap, searching for ones that promised more. The pile looked like Mount Wawalag, even to the shapes of the sisters on its peak.

"Follow Malgu River through Galwan country; it'll take you to *nongaru* Billabong—our womb. When you are there, call . . ."

An empty flagon skidded from the pile, rolled across the ground below and heading fast toward me broke against a wrecked car.

Plonk reached the summit and tried to hold onto one of the sisters, covered in bottles. He clung to a breast, but it snapped off and an empty flagon rolled down the slope. Suddenly the mountain burst, scattering broken glass over the ground. "*Warngi!*" called out Wagudi. The word meant a huge monster, not often seen in Galwan, but feared by every tribal soul.

The monster tottered over the rubbish dump, rattling and moving much like bulldozers do. On the metal beast rode Ranger dressed in the same clothes he had worn on the TV box. Ure grabbed for a spear and mounting it quickly on his thrower charged at the chest of the white man. The machine tilted its blade upward to shield the *balanda*; *gara* ("flint spearhead") thrust against metal, and two sparks bounced back. Wagudi rushed away looking for his *didjeridu*. The roar might frighten the monster if not tame it. The elder dashed inside the old car and peeped under the seat that I slept on. As he climbed out, his

29

head banged hard against the metal roof and he fell down on his back. He sat for a while nursing the bump on his head, while his eyes rested on *dugaruru*, which must have slipped out of the Hessian bag.

"It was given to me by my mother," I said.

"All women have it—it's your *marain*."

"What should I do with the stone?"

"It's to bring life to the Galwan country. You'll live to see it."

"Where should I keep the stone?"

"Your mother should have told you."

"Does it bring children?"

"How else would we be born? Hide it from the *balandas!*"

The elder put his hand on the stone, held it for a while and then walked slowly away from the wrecked car to search for his *didjeridu*. Outside, the noise of the crawling monster grew louder, the rattling changing into howling.

I woke up to see a man driving a Land Rover around the dump, his head poking out of the car window and calling out, "Stray cats, dogs and boongs—out!" He yells the warning three times, and then some noisy gear mounted on the back tray of the vehicle began pumping out a large gray jet of something that looked like both fume and liquid. A mask shields the driver's face, giving him the look of a malevolent spirit that has just emerged from our mythical past to hound tribal souls in the bush. I must rush to the discarded water tank several spears away. Plonk might still be asleep, and if he is not dragged out into the bush . . . those fumes would choke even a crocodile. Wait a moment—the Land Rover is just about to move behind a large heap of stale bread. It is much better not to be seen near it; though the stuff is on the refuse heap, the whites do not like you sniffing their food.

A large truck drives in, making the ground shiver. As it backs

30

up to the pile, part of the chassis springs up into the air like a propped-up goanna and a load slides down from its metal belly. Bones, dry and old, with chunks of soil stuck to them, rolled to the ground. Some had been partly broken, others crushed into a mass of splinters by some great force that had rolled over them. A red-haired truck driver shouts toward the Land Rover, "I brought you a whole pack of gins."

Chunks of old and weather-worn wood came down on the heap, too. There were blocks the size of fence posts, but carved some looked like . . . they must be *wuramu* ("poles") for sure. After a man dies, the elders erect one and they carve his *marain* ("totem") pattern and *babaru* ("family symbols") into the wood. It is all done to please the spirits of the one who has passed on and to make sure that once he reaches Bralgu to join the ancestors, he will be recognized by his tribal designs and welcomed. In Galwan the poles are erected in the bush at Mount Wawalag in the burial cave on a small plateau. It is a sacred place, and women are not allowed to go there. If any of us were seen, it would anger the spirits of the dead. "You could be speared for it," *momo* warned me. I should not look at *wuramu*—human or spirit. They are all our fellows and feel pain just the same.

The truck driver yells again, "Come and see the bloody gins."

I saw Plonk in the discarded water tank, only his head showing above the edge of the rusty container. His mouth was wide open, gasping for air not words this time. The truck, hardly a spear away, shielded him from the *balandas*, and though their voices could have been heard much farther away I doubt if any of it reached him. Run out, you fool!

The Land Rover stops behind the truck, and the dump's caretaker pulls off the mask. Near him, three skulls rolled down from the pile, soil falling from the hollows. "Those must have been the chief and his two wives."

31

A red-haired man leans out of the truck. "They're savages all right. The old doc says that the abos can put on clothes and wash every day, but their hearts stay in the bush."

The caretaker watches from his Land Rover as the skulls disappear into the bush below the dump. "They must have had a lot of women through the center."

"A whole graveyard of bloody gins. They served our prospectors and miners during the last mining rush. But not a single brat to show for it; I tell you, screwing a gin is like pouring into a tub."

"Sterile?"

The redheaded man wiped his mouth with an arm. "The abos breed differently. I know of only one man who makes brats with gins, one of us lot. The abos say that the spooks make the children, not man."

"It has something to do with a stone kept in a woman's womb, so I heard.

Redhead sneers. "The children hatch out from it, hmm!"

"Some kind of totem, I reckon."

The whites like to hold talk when they meet at the dump. Plonk thinks *balandas* hang around to boast about the piles of stale food and junk metal they can afford to chuck away. I wish Plonk was out of that tank. I think I just heard a bump; he might be struggling hard to get out. A man could easily suffocate from the fumes.

"Where did you hear that . . . about that stone?" asks Redhead.

"My padre told me. We were at the reserve during the war. He was well briefed, I gather."

"Gins might be stuffed with rocks for him; I hit the top of the hole of so many of them and never struck a bloody rock. Have you ever been at Gin Downs, mate?"

"No. That's a homestead up the river, near the reserve border?"

32

"It was a homestead till some fellows struck uranium west of there. That was years ago. Actually, we should have called the place Prospectors' Paradise."

"Did you strike it rich there?"

"Well, I was a young lad then—neither innocent nor virgin." Redhead got out of the truck holding a packet of tobacco. "Let's roll one. . . . Yeah, in the good old days we used to ride into the reserve, bring out a whole flock of young gins, and chain the lot to a big tree."

The man opposite him looked blank. "What for?"

"You have to strangle the snake that lays the eggs."

"What about chucking some arsenic into the water hole. My padre says many tribes were wiped out that way."

Redhead bit off the loose end of his cigarette. "You have to do the job and have fun as well. That padre of yours, did he ever tell you about the Grand National?"

The caretaker raised his eyebrows: "You mean races, I never thought you had any racehorses here?"

"We had the races. The people used to flock from the whole bush to see them—prospectors, stockmen; they all came."

"What did you race with—mules or camels?"

"We had gins. They race well if you know how to keep them hot. My friend, an old chap called Dusty, he was bloody good at that."

The caretaker preferred silence.

Plonk has slid back into the shelter; only his hand shows over the edge, trying to grip the metal. It will be boiling hot in that rusty container, much more so than in the wreck here. I must get him out.

The caretaker puffed out smoke, glancing at Redhead. "What about your boss . . . would the old doc have some wild stories to tell?"

"My word he does. When he was in the bush he knocked off a daughter or a wife of one of those boong chiefs."

The caretaker said slowly, "They befriended him before that, as far as I know."

"Of course they did. He took part in all the initiation rituals; breaking all those young gins with boomerangs before screwing them. That man, he left behind a whole flock of half-caste brats. Look, he's the only one of us the gins bore from, bloody fanny."

"Padre! Did he really?"

"You're new here, of course. When they struck it rich west of Gin Downs, that parochial fool sided with the bloody blacks!"

"Was he complaining about the mining or the screwing of the gins?"

"He made a fuss about everything. The screwing at Gin Downs went on for years before the mining boom. My friend Dusty would have so many notches on his belt . . . By Jove, that belt would have to be miles long for all those gins."

I hope the whites will keep on talking until I read that discarded water tank. No, don't rush—crawl slowly, like a blue-tongued lizard. That truck will shield me soon.

"Are there many abos down at the center now?" asks the caretaker.

"There's a few scared survivors; old doc experiments on them. We're called the Centre for Human Development now."

"You've been improving that place lately. The old doc must have a few bob to spare."

"Adder foots the bill. They're making a fortune out in the bush. When they spit we can all bathe in it. Uranium, that stuff they're mining there, is as pricy as gold."

Yes, I am safer here. The tank is not far off now. I have to crawl a short distance only, but there is nothing around to hide me from view and . . . A rat rattles over a corrugated metal sheet, runs over to a pile of dumped bones and dashes behind a skull. Wait for a while—both men are looking this way.

34

The caretaker tosses his cigarette butt toward the pile. "Haven't they made some sort of treaty, some kind of law to keep the whites from the reserve. Old Doc Cross saw to it, so I heard."

Redhead shouts, "Law my arse. That mining went on twenty-odd years ago. The world suddenly had enough uranium to make all the bombs it needed, so we had to close. If it hadn't been for that, we would have mined the last boulder in the reserve."

The hot air in the tank smells acid. Whatever Plonk had drunk has knocked him hard. His limbs feel slimy and heavy; as I drag him out, one of his legs slips from my hand and drums against the corrugated iron.

The caretaker mumbles, "Bloody dingoes, sneaking in and out. They don't seem to mind this bloody chemical I spray the place with."

Redhead still claps his hand, chasing a persistent fly. "I'll be off to the bush shortly, into the reserve again."

"Is Doctor Cross going back?"

"No, I'll be working for his junior, that Adder bloke. They need someone who can handle boongs well."

"They struck it rich here—hills of uranium, I gather."

"Much, much richer find than that at Gin Downs, mate. A lump of that bloody stuff, no bigger than a billycan, could blast a whole . . ." Redhead raises both hands and, struggling for an appropriate word, mumbles, ". . . a whole country, I reckon."

The caretaker wipes his dry lips. "Such a rich find on abo's land."

Redhead swipes at his face with a hand, and the buzzing of the fly stops. "Look, the only land the black man has is the dirt under his fingernails—dinkum, mate."

"Don't let your boss hear that one."

"To hell with that fool—the boongs have no right to those

35

rocks. It was a white hand that made the world, mate."

"I might drop into the center to see Cross; he was my padre during the war—a very just chap."

A short silence sat between the two men, then Redhead broke into a laugh. "Old doc—a padre. What about that!"

I have to drag Plonk slowly over the ground littered with broken bottles and pieces of rusting metal. There are some bushes on the fringes of the dump where he can lie in the shade while I dash down to the river to get some water. The whites might be here for a while. It is not the best place for a chat, but when that lot begin to swap stories about us, no flies or bad smells will drive them off.

CHAPTER FIVE

There must be a safe hiding place for *dugaruru*. For the last few days I have carried the stone with me wrapped in a Hessian bag. At night I kept it under my head as a cushion to be sure no one took it away.

Across the river, directly opposite the rubbish dump and our camp, a huge concrete pipe springs out from the bank. Perhaps it comes all the way from town? The green bushes and vines concealing the entrance, the place seems to have been forgotten by the whites but is known to animals and to some of us looking for a safe shelter. Wagudi used to hide his *didjeridu* there, and when he was being hounded, Ure often sneaked inside, too.

Something is moving ahead of me. No, it couldn't be my shadow—it is much farther inside the tunnel than that. "Being here is like being at your own *babaru*," Ure told me in the tunnel once before. The *balandas* used to search the camp and the rubbish dump, but they never looked in the pipe.

From up ahead comes the sound of flapping wings; it must be a bird. A *lindarid* cockatoo had flown inside just before I entered and . . . Look, the bird's silhouette moves slowly along the wall.

37

If you are not tall and can bend easily, you can walk instead of crawl through the tube. It is the middle of the Dry now; the rain has not come for quite a while, and the patches of fine sand gathered in the bottom of the pipe have almost dried out. Someone has passed through, leaving behind the prints of bare feet. It looks . . . yes, I know the marks! You can tell people by their tracks just as you can by their voice or face, and you recognize not only relatives but any human who has something of his own. The elders can tell black man's *mala* ("clan") and *mada* ("tongue") by looking at his footprints, and "Marngit, our medicine man, could even see the track of a spirit," my *momo* told me.

The bird's silhouette holds still on the wall; it seems to wait for me to catch up. My eyes have grown used to the dark now. Those footprints in the sand look shallower than mine. She must have been very light, she took short steps, the way people do when they age and . . . look, she was not walking straight; perhaps she was suffering from thirst, no—hunger, more likely. When you do not eat for several days your knees grow weak and you sway when you walk. The big toe of her right foot must have been hurt, swollen I'd say; she kept it above the ground and touched the sand only now and then when she was moving across the sandy humps. It looks as though she had been down to the river and then headed back to the shelter again; perhaps she had to go out to look for yams . . . no, she must have been after yabbies. Poor soul, she must have lost nearly all her teeth—the yabby claws have been thrown away; it is the best part, but only if you can chew.

The cockatoo has moved on but stops again; it will wait, I need not hurry. Under my foot . . . *maidja*, the "breast girdle"! The strings look worn, they crumple in my fingers. When she is aged, however, a woman no longer needs them. She has also left behind a small depression in the sand where she rested and . . . yes, she had to struggle to stand up again, pressing her hands against the ground to force her worn-out body up. Look, she had long, fine fingers, good for plunging into mud holes when you have to get yabbies out of their hideouts. It appears as if she had only one hand; the other seems to have been cut off at the wrist. Instead of the print of the fingers and palm on the sand, only the mark of the bone where the wound had healed shows. She struggled for a while but not for long and then . . . poor soul, she had to come down on her knees and elbows and crawl forward for a few more spears. The bird screeches; it grows restless and stretches both wings. I doubt the *balandas* would come down here, though if anyone is about, *lindarid* would be quicker in telling it than humans.

Here mother rested again and left both *galamba*, her "armbands." A dilly bag is here too, hers? I am as sure of it as I am of my own skin. My *momo* told me that in Galwan a woman keeps the souls of her children in *badi*, a bag like this, and she often carries it hanging around her neck for the little ones to feel the warmth of her breast. I never learned how long she has to hold them close to her, but when they are young the little souls have to be shielded day and night.

Down the tunnel drifts a constant humming. It must come from outside. I heard the same noise when I was here to see Ure. He told me that the town is more than a voice away, but the whites are a loud lot and they keep reminding you of their presence wherever you happen to be.

There is not much in mother's *badi*; a piece of stone that looks like glass, a bone knife, a bit of string and *dudji*, the pair of "fire sticks." That leaves plenty of room for the souls of children to fit in. Do the little souls talk? My *momo* said you can hear them chatting from the bag, especially the girls. A mother teaches them all there is to know until they are taken by *duwei*, their "husband." The girls have to learn about the right way to bring up children of their own; she tells them that, too. It is not just the giving birth, as the *balandas* might think; the woman has to know the right time to let the spirit from Bralgu, or one from the sacred water hole, bring a child into her *walg*, ("womb") and . . . how do the spirits get inside? There must be something else—I have been told so little of what a woman should know.

Down the long passage drifts the noise of trucks rattling along the road above. The tunnel leads into a short passage only to end up against a concrete wall. "Kangaroo's pouch," Ure calls this dark corner. It is a long time since he sheltered here. I had to call in often with food and water, for he is the young brother of Bungul, who was my husband-to-be. Even if it had not been for that, you would not let a wounded soul suffer pain. I brought him a bundle of leafy branches to wave and keep *wurulu* off his face: flies can smell blood from the far end of the tunnel. The monsoon rains have come since and swept the place. Feel! A stone is half buried in the sand, the one I brought from the river to break his food, because when your face is covered with wounds, your jaws are too stiff to chew.

Balandas smell—it is not only their skin but the soap they use and the food they eat. Ure could even tell how many of the whites were hounding him by sniffing that stuff they put on their faces when they shave. Is there a gap farther up the tunnel to let the air in? Yes, there is a light coming from above; the grille on the main shaft has been removed and I can squeeze out through the opening. Move slowly; the whites are good at setting traps. "You learn that when it is too late to go back," I heard Wagudi tell Ure once. Tiptoe slowly now. I must have come out into one of the buildings down in the town, because the air smells strongly of tobacco and grog.

A big crowd of people has gathered here in a dimly lit hall; the whites must be having one of their ceremonies, the ones where they group together indoors to chant and sing, if not to booze and argue. They often ring church bells to call on their big boss, Jesus or Justice. No, the place could not be a church; a man is standing in the middle of the hall on a square platform rigged with thick ropes. A blaze of light is beamed onto his face, and he is holding up one of his hands to shield his eyes.

"Ladies and gents, welcome to our Adder Championship of the year. And now, our sponsor . . ."

It is Redhead from the rubbish dump; his clothes are different, but his voice is the same. He is wearing a shirt, but as he tries to shield his eyes from the light, one sleeve slips back to show a tattooed cross over one wrist. A huge dog on a lead is brought to him; the man props up the animal on his hind legs and slowly turns it around to make sure that no one in the hall misses seeing the beast.

"Proudly presenting to you: an Alsatian called Progress, the holder of the Governor Arthur Cross and the winner of many contests. He used to be in our service up at Gin Downs."

Progress is led to a corner of the ring, a large medal jingling from his collar. The animal turns around to face the crowd, opens his jaws showing most of his teeth, then sits as told.

A bald man, partly cutting off my view of the ring, shouts: "Hey, that couldn't be Dusty's dog, Cheat!"

"Let it be, Stumpy," says a man with thick curly hair next to him.

"Dusty's dog would be too old now even to pee. Bloody Cheat."

"It's all in fun. What did that beast do up at Gin Downs, anyway?" The curly-haired man has a young but husky voice.

Redhead comes up again. "Another challenger: a dingo called Woolly, comes straight from the bush. He has survived many traps and is on top of the wanted list. Don't point your finger, he'll snap it off. As old Doctor Cross says, 'You can't kill

41

the spirit of the bush.' "

Poor Muru lies flat on the floor hoping not to be seen. They have placed his cage in one of the corners. I had better move closer to the ring so that he can see me; with a bit of luck I might be able to poke my hand through the bars of the cage and scratch him behind the ears; he likes that. I'll have to be careful not to rub hard and harm the tender skin infested by mange.

The bald man made his way to the ring. "From Gin Downs, hmm? Was he there on Her Majesty's Service?" he sneered.

Both men have opened cans of beer. "What did he do there that was so great, anyway?"

"But that beast was never there, I can bloody tell."

The dogs are set free, but Muru does not want to come out; he cowers up against the mesh, his limbs stiff and shivering. Redhead flicks a cigarette lighter and brings the flame right up against the red skin. Muru shoots out of the cage and as soon as he sets paw in the ring Progress throws him down on the floor, tears a chunk of skin from his shoulder and then goes for his neck.

"What a queer one; it couldn't even stay on its feet." The curly-haired youth's voice sounds even huskier.

"I reckon he grew up on the rubbish dump." Stumpy scratched his bald head with the edge of the can before sipping his drink.

"We pay to see a good fight, not a bloody cur."

"It's a charity contest, sonny—just like the ones they bloody tricked us into in the old days."

Curly wiped his lips, wet from the drink. "The old doc must have skinned that cur to make a few bob extra for his boongs."

I still have to find my way to the corner where Muru's cage is; it is not far, just on the opposite side of the ring. I had better crawl so that I will not be caught by the spotlights. The fight has stopped, perhaps for a short break. The two men can still be heard.

"That dog used to take care of gins when they 'rotted.' He never fought." Stumpy's voice grows cold.

"How could a girl 'rot'?"

"The way those blokes carried on up there, no woman could last for long."

Poor Muru lies on the floor of the cage licking his wounds. I can hear his heart thumping like the pounding of a parrot's beak on a hollow log. The jaws of the *balanda* beast have left hardly any of his skin intact. I whisper a few words to let him know that I am close by. There is a good gap between the bars of the cage, and I pass my hand in to scratch the poor fellow behind the ears. Muru leans against my arm and sighs deeply. Someone from the crowd throws a few darts toward us; one lands on the cage floor and the other against the steel bars. At first I thought the dog would growl or bark, but instead he kept panting and only his snout and whiskers twitched angrily.

The crowd howls as the fight begins again; Muru must have sensed that I could not help and he seemed to know that if there was to be a way out he must make it for himself. Without being thrown, he lies down on his back and waits for the weight of Progress's body to come down on him; then, struggling from underneath, he twists his head behind the Alsatian's back legs.

"Bloody cheat!" Tossing his can, Stumpy splashes the dogs with the beer.

Losing no time, Muru snatches the balls of his opponent, ripping them off.

Progress gives the snarl of a mortally wounded animal, jerks up in the air several times and falls over the edge of the ring. The crowd is howling, eager to see what is happening to Progress and no one looks at Muru dashing to me; I hold him tightly in my arms and head quickly out of the hall. Luckily the lights are dim and the tunnel is not far off.

It seems much darker in the tunnel now, the air thicker; still it is safer here than outside. Ure thought so, too. "They can't see

43

black skin when you hide in the dark," he told me when I last saw him here. He had handcuffs around one of his wrists, and the skin had toughened under the metal band like the sole of a foot. He often ground the iron against that stone I had brought him, but not all stones are good for filing. Come on, Muru, let us move on a bit farther; the blacks are not the only ones who feel safer here.

Down at the river end of the tunnel a glimmer of light is showing. Surely we are not there already; the tunnel had seemed much longer on the way here. I often had to stop and catch my breath then. I might have taken a different way this time, a shortcut, perhaps. But, no, this pipe is like the belly of a snake—you can only go forward or backward, and if the whites come from both directions you are trapped.

Ure might be back hiding here again; it is a long time, a whole Wet season, since I last saw him. Those handcuffs must be off by now; there is a place up the river, a tough slab of rock, that our people use to sharpen their stone axes and spear blades on. "No steel could hold out against that one," Ure hoped. That is where he must have gone.

Yes, they are coming, I can see the light of a torch floating in the dark like a distant star. They are moving in from both ends, but the *balandas* must be a good way off because I cannot hear them; it will not be for long. Muru has sensed them already. He is too weak to claw me or squeal but has just enough strength to prick up his ears. I can feel both of them spring up in the air, listening to the noise that is too distant for humans to hear. I had better sit down and let them come to me instead of trying to run. If I let Muru go, the dog might be able to sneak past them and find his way out. But he is too weak for that now, poor soul; he can only walk on three legs and weaves from one side of the pipe to the other. Since we left the hall I have had to carry him much of the way, and it will be days before he is well enough to run again.

44

I can hear them now, not the steps or the voices but a metallic jingling that sounds like the rattling of a loose chain. I once heard Ure telling the other fellows that when the *balandas* chase a man, they do not talk; they have no voices at all, they just whistle and jingle their handcuffs. It must be so. Ure should know better than any of us; you see him in the camp one day, and then the whole season might go by before he appears again. No one asks much about it; we all know that he is either on the run or in the lockup. And whichever way it goes, it will end up the same. Whenever the *balandas* were out looking for him, Wagudi used to sit for hours behind the bamboo clumps by the river and, raising *bilma* ("clapping sticks") toward the horizon, chant endlessly. He is not *marngit*, to sing out *dal* ("magic power"), but he knows the right words to call for help. The spirits in Bralgu would have liked it and come. I doubt if Ure will ever be back; when he was at the slab to cut the handcuffs, he must have been told to stay in the bush.

There is a good heap of sand here that has piled up. I must hurry and bury Muru; he can hide there while they take me away, then crawl down to the river and go bush to look for Ure. Muru will make it. I will dig the hole right against the wall so the *balandas* will not tread on him when they come after me.

CHAPTER SIX

The whites always make enclosures from metal; it is much tougher than the stuff they build their houses from, and when you are locked inside there is no hope of grinding your way out.

I cannot see the sky; instead, high above us arches a structure of heavy metal girders and thick mesh. From here it looks like a mangrove forest stripped of its leaves. Birds and animals are often boxed up like this. They are kept in captivity so that they will reveal the secrets of their lives in the bush, but most of them, except the parrots, die rather than talk. Wagudi thinks that, too: "They've got us all in."

Old Gunbuna mumbles through his beard, "They grabbed the country, now they're after our souls, too." I doubt that he will ever say a word to Cross again.

"The *balandas* were always after our girls before. Why have they caged us?"

The two elders sit on a log. On the ground down here the compound hardly looks like an enclosure; if you do not think about it, the place could be mistaken for the bush. The bars, painted green, are well concealed behind the bushes. There are some trees too; nothing much grows on them. The trunks and branches are made of funny colored fibers, bits of cotton wool are painted to look like moss and the leaves do not bend. There is a bird with wings outstretched floating in the air between the top twigs of the trees and the mesh above it. Since I first saw it days ago, the bird has not moved. In the branched fork of one of the trees rests *djanda* ("goanna"), with a wide, fat belly and an ash-colored skin without a shine. Yesterday Wagudi threw a pebble and hit it on the leg, but the reptile did not even flick its tongue out. Now he looks at the metal forest above. "If we could only turn into flies or midges we could get through."

"That might happen yet, I sent a call for help to Bralgu."

"Let's hope our spirit ancestors will not keep this curse on us forever."

Gunbuna raises his bushy gray eyebrows. "What curse?"

Wagudi moves his lips silently, as though munching his words to feel whether they are too hard. "We shouldn't let Cross and that son of his, Ranger, on *nongaru*. The *balandas* had no business initiating our girls."

It looks as though Gunbuna has just swallowed an anteater. "I thought they were our friends," he says, and walks away.

There is a tree almost in the middle of the enclosure; I do not remember seeing it anywhere before. The branches are weighed down with fruit of a strange shape—the size of a mango but round and red, perhaps a desert apple. The tree does not grow in Galwan country, but I remember seeing it somewhere. Gunbuna might know; I had better ask him. The old man now sits in the shade of a bush, sharpening *galdj* ("stone ax"). He has been doing it on and off for days, ever since they brought me here. Next to him is a coconut shell that holds water to wet the stone and make the rubbing smoother; it is empty now, and the old man looks at the dry blade, then spits on it instead.

The old men are not to be disturbed. Gunbuna hates to be

47

troubled and looks at me angrily. I'll ask him about my mother; he will understand that better and be eager to chat because she was born *dua* and *mugul*, a kind of niece, to him. "How did she get out of here?" I lowered my voice almost to a whisper.

He looked at the empty coconut shell. "She was already gone when they brought me in."

"There must be a way out somewhere." The enclosure, about a stone's throw wide and a good voice long, is stretched along the side of an L-shaped yellow building, backing onto the shorter wing. A barred gate separates the two with a shutter let into it that opens at the white man's will.

Gunbuna spat on the ax to wet the blade. "She turned into a cockatoo."

"Why?"

"It's our totem; many women do it. Our fellows watched from down here while she crawled up the mesh, using her claws and beak. See that funneled entrance halfway up the wall; she swung around it and then flew off to Bralgu."

I whisper, "She came to see me."

The old man held his thumb against the blade to test the sharpness of the ax. "They always do—don't tell the *balanda* about it."

What does he need the ax for; there is no hope of hunting here. I should not be laughing about it, for he is a tribal elder and older than any other man. "Would mother go back to our country?"

"They always do."

"It is too far to come."

"Our world is never far away, not for a woman."

"Why especially for us?"

Around Gunbuna's head a belt, woven with various colors and tribal patterns but almost worn out, has slid down to his eyebrows. He pushes it up. "The women are *marain*. Only they

48

can bear the children."

"The men make . . . they make the ceremonies, erect *murlg* the 'huts,' hunt . . ."

"They have to be born first. With no children born, Narku and Galwan—both tribes will die out. It's up to you and the spirits to see that they live." Unhappy with the blunt blade, he bent down to keep on rubbing the ax.

I have taken the empty shell and brought some water, but I doubt that he noticed me going and coming back. He forces his ax against a piece of wood to test the blade, dreaming, perhaps, of building a hut. He will help make one for me when I have children. "How many saplings do you need for a *murlg*?"

"It all depends how big the *babaru* ["family"] is."

He should know how big the family is going to be—his son, Warinji, me and a few children. The Galwan women never have many; no one ever told me why—the tribal country is vast. "Would it help if the tribe were bigger; there is so much land there?"

"There has to be room for trees, birds and animals—they're our people reborn."

He might live with us, but for a while only. Gunbuna will stay mostly at Mount Wawalag and be with his brother, Marngit, our medicine man. The two seldom part.

Pressed hard, the ax squeaks against the rubbing stone.

"Here, have some water."

Gunbuna glances at the shell and spits on the stone again.

The old man will be angry with me. He knows who gives us water, food and dry wood to make a fire to gather around—just as we did in the bush. Last evening I had a whole kangaroo limb cooked in hot ashes; he shouted when I tried to give it to him.

At first I thought he might be angry because I was taken from Galwan by Ranger and did not stay there to marry Bungul. Then Wagudi told me later, "He wants nothing that comes

49

from Doctor Cross—that *balanda* tricked us all."

Doctor Cross is too old to run around and hunt, but Redhead might do that for him, or maybe the doctor's son, Ranger, sends the meat here. He is the one who knows every bird, animal and reptile and can tell where they are hiding. When he was in Galwan country he knew every tree by its name and could speak our lingo as well as any black fellow. He only got strange when he began to chip off the rocks and gather the pieces in a big knapsack that he carried on his back all the time. Everyone thought that his boss, that Jesus or Justice Man, had sung some power, like our *dal*, to put a curse on him for initiating the tribal girls at *nongaru*.

The rubbing stone squeaks—an insect caught in a burning log.

"All that is here comes from the *balanda*. If I ever escape I shall sneak you some food and water through the fence."

The rubbing gets quicker. What did that dreadful white man do to all of us? Gunbuna will not say a word. I shall ask others as well about my mother; there are a handful of old men here, almost all of them Galwan and Narku. I am the only woman. Some of the fellows hide in the bushes during the day; poor souls, they must be right out of the bush. In the evening, they grow braver and come out of hiding. We all group together in front of the steel gate and watch Redhead through the bars wheeling a trolley loaded with the carcass of a wallaby or an emu if we are lucky; he passes the food to us through the shutter.

Lucky Ure to be free, for though handcuffed, he can gather food of his own in the bush.

They dig a deep, wide hole that looks like an empty pool at one end of the enclosure. At first no one wondered what the *balanda* might use the pit for. For so long life had gone the way the whites wanted it, and to worry about what is to come could only

50

cause us anxiety. The men, however, suddenly grow restless, as if the hole is going to hatch a monster that will crawl out during the night and swallow us all. More than any of the other men, Gunbuna feels burdened by fear and he hangs around, peering into the pit from behind the bushes. "Big *ingabunga*, I have seen holes like this before."

"When?" asked Dadangu.

"During that first mining madness—'bust,' they call it."

"It's called boom," Dadangu corrected the old man.

"Yes, they dug some nasty *ingabunga*. Then it's hard to tell what was worst, the poisoned water hole or that ditch," worries Wagudi.

Gunbuna's cheek trembled like the tail of a wounded lizard. "They set the whole bush ablaze. From one end of the sky to the other, instead of your country you see a mountain of flame."

Dadangu scratches his head. "Why would they burn the bush?"

"To expose the rocks, kill plants and animals—everything that is in the white man's path," explains Wagudi.

"Did they really mine at Galwan?"

That lad is a fool—he is annoying both the old men.

Wagudi's voice grows edgy. "They did a lot of prospecting throughout the rescue; Galwan is a big country, they caused great harm."

Gunbuna tries to wet his dry lips with his tongue. "That mountain of flame kept rolling toward us, every day a voice or two closer. Haven't you seen the scarred country?"

I saw it, the burned hills covered with sooty rocks. I was with Ranger then, heading from our country to the white man's world, and I knew of no proper word to ask why the hills were coated with black.

They wait for Dadangu to say something, then Wagudi breaks the silence. "The trees might never grow there again.

51

The plants are like humans; they spread the word about what happened, and . . . you wouldn't like to be burned twice from the same hand."

When we were with Ranger, we passed through a whole plain of skeleton trees. So tall they looked sky-high but were only dry trunks. We spoke no word. Yes, he too must have felt scared of dead trees, each one so much bigger than a human.

"What did the fire have to do with *ingabunga*, those holes, anyway?" Dadangu grows irritated.

"When a man stands up for his country, that is where he ends," says Gunbuna slowly.

Dadangu sneeringly looks at Gunbuna. "How were the men buried in the pits—dead or alive?"

"Whichever way it pleased the whites; then they packed in soil or sometimes they brought loads of rocks and dumped them on top of the bodies."

"They often poured concrete over them—that is the worst; no spirit could ever find its way out then." Wagudi's face looks stone-hard.

Gunbuna blinks, his eyes wet. "The fellows called out many times in my dream, asking for help. They had to get to Bralgu, our spirit world. They ask me to plead for them with Marngit, my brother."

I was often told of a large pit in the west part of Galwan, sealed with concrete that no soul could get out of. Our fellows tried to break the cover; men from neighboring tribes came to help, but there is little a stone or a club in your hands can do against concrete. A big ceremony was held, followed by a whole chain of them, with Marngit calling "Bugalili" for days from Mount Wawalag, hoping to bring help.

"Didn't Cross help to stop the *balanda?*" asks Dadangu. The men looked at Gunbuna; silence fell.

My *momo* says that the voice of her brother grew hoarse from

52

long calls and might not have reached Bralgu, but it reached sky for sure. *Djanbuwaul*, Thunder Man, the mightiest of all our ancestors, rode in on a stormy cloud from the sea. He was full of anger, they say, tearing the sky apart as he waved *larban* ("magic spear"). That was a good blow; it lit up the whole sky, split a large tree, ripped it out of the earth and broke the nearby concrete slab in two.

Now Gunbuna lowered his voice. "That mighty ancestor could melt steel."

"Have you called to him?" Dadangu still spoke loudly.

"Marngit, my brother, will do that. Wait until Ure reaches him."

"Will Ure . . ."

A sudden cough from Wagudi warned both men to say no more.

Plonk wants to say something; he twitches the corner of his mouth and knocks *bilma* against his head; I think one bit means "yes" and two means "no." What could he know about the boom and the people buried in the ditch when he is younger than I. Mother had him after she left our country, some years after that mining madness subsided.

"U-u-u-ure!" Plonk stands up and, straightening his shoulder, raises his right hand to show how good Ure is at throwing the spear. Did anyone ever tell him that I am his sister? Wagudi would have been the one to tell him about it, though I doubt that he revealed much. Plonk hangs around the whites more than any of us do; when we were at the camp by the river the *balandas* often came looking for him, always carrying a flagon or two of grog. Perhaps the spirits thought he was put among us by the whites to hear what we talk about and gather all the secrets from the tribal elders and then pass it all on to the *balandas*. He must have done something wrong, even if he did not want to; being drunk makes men's minds go blind . . . and then an angry spirit took his head and twisted his mouth around so that he could not talk. Wagudi is sure it could not be anything else but that.

With them sits Gara, a fellow whose bushy hair looks like clumps of spinifex. When he moves, limping on one foot, the growth on his head sways, as thought it is caught in a breeze. The hair looks as if it is hiding one of his ears, but it is not there at all, and gone with it also is a chunk of the left side of his face, leaving behind a red patch of tender skin. When you talk to Gara, he has to turn his one remaining ear to the speaker to hear the words, but that only helps a bit. He is not from our tribal country, and he speaks a lingo no one knows much about, though he seems to know the white man's words well.

The *balanda* have dripping skin; Redhead, Stumpy and the caretaker have all come inside to labor and sweat. Even that curly-haired lad is in the enclosure, blistering his palms on the shovel handle. "What about putting those boongs on, they've got muscles?" He wipes the soil from his panting mouth.

"They're not supposed to dig—all the thoroughbreds." Redhead waits for a while before adding, ". . . the old doc says so."

Curly frowns, making a silent complaint.

"They have to save their strength for a more fertile task," says his mate, Stumpy, who then turns to the caretaker. "Do you think it'll work, this business—breeding a new race?"

Redhead interrupts. "You're all going to be paid for this job, so get on with it."

They are mad. The sun has gone high and the day feels very hot; even a hounded dingo would head for shade. Why dig the ground; doing that you rip the belly of your mother, so our elders say.

Curly, still troubled by the soil on his mouth, spits. "Did you have to make a hole like this at Gin Downs?"

"We had a billabong right at the homestead. You just unchain the gins and chuck them in." Redhead smiles.

The curly-haired lad looks blank.

"They toss them in to wash off the blood," explains Stumpy.

"Blood, from what?"

"We're never short of it, not at the Grand National. Once the chaps made a raid deep into the reserve and brought out a whole pack of girls ritually decorated—seized them just before they were to be initiated and . . . terribly young. Most of them had not yet properly grown their 'black lawn,' as old Dusty called the virgin hair. He knew quite a few ways to make them bleed. The blood excites men. Don't you think so, Stumpy?" Redhead looks at him suddenly.

"What?"

"Blood is sexy; it was especially so at the Grand National."

The bald man frowns. "I took no part in your bloody races."

"Come on, mate, you placed your bet now and then."

The men must be able to see me. I am only a short distance away resting in the shade of a bush. The *balandas* speak loudly; they can be heard in just about every part of the enclosure. Even Wuluru could hear them if her windows were open.

Curly leans on the shovel handle. "What did you bet on, anyway?"

No one must have asked that before, and it took Redhead a while to say, "Well, you bet how many times a man was going to screw or how many times a gin would 'come' or how many men she'd last."

"You had a lot more games, then, than what I heard," says the caretaker.

"Actually, old Dusty was very inventive; he always came up with a new idea. He ran the whole show there, you know."

Momo told me of that place. She did not speak of all that went on there, but she told me enough to warn me to keep away from the *balandas*.

55

Curly keeps his mouth open wide. "Anyway, that large dog of Dusty's, what did he have to do up there?"

They all keep quite for a while, then Redhead speaks. "You can teach a dog to do anything."

Stumpy was about to say something but turned without a word. He sits down on the bank of red soil freshly dug from the hole. "Why not tell the lad all of it?" He looks back at Redhead. "What about that scar on your lip, hmm?"

"A bloody gin bit me. They were often wild, would snap at you like a dingo. Poor Dusty, one nipped off half his lip. Actually, I was the screwing champion. Old Dusty saw to it. He always had a skink at hand—a small burrowing fella."

"You slipped that inside a gin?"

"That makes a helluva difference when you screw in a contest."

"Would she let you do it?"

"They're chained. Besides, you give the gin a bottle of grog and you can mess with her body at will. That skink, my God, that was . . ."

Stumpy looks at him again. "Do you really have one?"

The men are silent. From some distance away comes the squeaky sound of the rubbing stone as Gunbuna sharpens his ax, but that soon fades away.

The caretaker sits down next to Stumpy. "I gather it makes no difference if an abo dies from a poisoned water hole or is chucked into a billabong to be fed to the crocodiles or is stuffed with a skink. . . . Even this cage built here. Mate, I mean —it's death just the same."

"I wonder what our old padre Cross would say to that?" Stumpy has a lump of red soil in his hand and, crushing it suddenly, he watches the clumps of earth fall to the ground.

The tender skin around the missing ear could be from a

56

machete cut; only sharp steel and a fast hand could make such a wound.

"I have a friend—they're after him, too." I leaned toward the unscarred side of Gara's face.

Gara sits in a corner of the enclosure. It looks as though he is dozing off, but he comes to life too soon for that. "You are from Narku, Ure's tribe."

"I will go to live there when I marry."

"Very brave young fellow," whispered the man.

"You know him!"

Gara closes his eyes again. Perhaps he does not like me asking about Ure. Why not tell me; we are alone—our fellows have dispersed to hide among the bushes. Some distance away Redhead still digs the pit, but he is too busy to hear the words.

One of Gara's eyes opens slightly, and with it comes a whisper. "He'll be all right."

The wound on his face looked very messy the day Redhead brought him in his Land Rover—inflamed and swollen. Much of it had subsided under a heavy coat of red mercury—the stuff Wuluru likes to splash over every wound. "I say, it heals nicely."

"It's an old scar, hurt again." A corner of his mouth twitched. It looks as if he is about to smile, but he stops suddenly, struck by sudden pain. He must have done the same when Wuluru tried to help him out of the Land Rover the day they brought him in. I watched them from here through the mesh of the enclosure, hardly a few paces away. "What have they done to you?" Her voice trembled. She was going to comfort him when Redhead warned, "Be careful. This one is quite wild—might have your hand off."

"He's waking up. He had a shock."

"I didn't hit him hard. C'mon, squirt him with that bloody needle."

57

Wuluru put away the injection. "He needs no tranquilizer."

"He's wild, I'm telling you. I trapped him in a cave."

Now Gara glances at me with a half-open eye. "Nice country you have up here in the bush; head for it when you get out of here."

"Who told you about Galwan?"

Gara keeps silent for a while. "That old fellow Gunbuna."

How could they have talked, the old man hardly knows a word of English. In the bush, he spoke with Cross often, but always in the tribal lingo.

A fly falls on Gara's wound, and he chases it off with his hand. "The *balandas* have long ears," he whispers.

Would Wuluru let him get out of here; she might. That day, when he was brought in, she yelled to Redhead, "Hurry up with that bloody trolley, the flies are swarming around him."

Redhead felt no hurry. "It's not the boong they wanted. He'll make up the number, anyhow. Besides, there are so few abos left to choose from."

"Bring that bloody trolley closer."

"All right, sweetie. Let's chuck him in."

The man wheeled the trolley, hitting the doorway.

"You . . . take care!" shouted Wuluru.

"Don't tell me he's one of your thoroughbreds."

"Gently, I said." Her voice rose higher.

Now leaning against the fence inside the enclosure, Gara gently passes his fingers over the wound to feel his healing skin.

"Has she known you for long?"

"She might have known a man that looked like me." His throat must feel dry.

"When they brought you in I thought it was one of our fellows."

Gara opens both eyes to check if Redhead is still busy digging.

58

"You thought it was Ure," he whispers.

"Surely you know him!"

"We were trapped in a cave together—up in the hills. I was getting sick and had to walk out to be captured. It did the trick; the *balanda* thought there was only one of us. They never went inside to search. That was days ago."

He looks toward Redhead again, as the white man wipes sweat from his forehead, and whispers, "I hope Ure frees himself from those manacles." His eyes close again.

They have stopped digging the hole; now they are smoothing the edges of the pit and throwing sand over them as if to make the ground feel softer. Redhead and his men drag a sheet of tough, green plastic to the pit and are trying to lay it flat on the bottom. I wonder if they did the same to those other holes they dug long ago during that mining boom.

"Will you pour concrete over us when we're buried?"

Redhead glances at me. "No one is going to be buried."

"They did it before."

"Maybe convicts did . . . or the first settlers; it's not done now. We are going to bring your tribe back to life again. The old doc is ready to program your breeding pattern; he hopes to do something about your color as well." Redhead stares at me. "You don't look as dark as the others."

I might be a bit lighter than mother but not nearly as light as Plonk. The exact shade of the skin does not worry any of us. Why do the *balandas* have to fuss about it?

"We're making a billabong here; she'll look like a real one. With luck I might be able to start filling her up the day after tomorrow."

"Is it . . ."

"It's all for your mob. The old doc'll be coming with his

59

magic stick to help get things going. You're going to have a bit of fun . . . the only woman among them!"

Redhead stops working for a while and measures me with his eyes; so does his working mate, that curly lad. I am not wearing any clothes—none of us do—and am even without a small rag to cover *diridiri*, the "pubic hair." Some days ago we were each given a cloth made from plastic sheeting; it was meant to look like the ones we had in the bush, which were woven from sea-gull feathers and bark softened by chewing. Wurulu calls the cloth *lap-lap*; it is not a Galwan word and does not sound like one of the white's either. The cover is uncomfortable, too; the plastic heats up quickly in the sun and feels . . . it almost burns your belly during the day, and at night it is hard and stone-stiff. The men threw off their coverings, nor do I wear mine any longer. Redhead stares at my *diridiri*. "A nice, curly patch you've got there, your 'black lawn,' as my old friend Dusty called it. You know, that bloke had a part of his lip bitten off; he used to get a hair between his teeth without opening his mouth. Whenever he pulled one, he felt like he was striking it rich."

"I thought he wasn't a prospector," said Curly.

"No, that bloke had more sense than to struggle through the bush searching for bloody uranium rocks. I hung around the homestead helping him." Redhead looks at me again. "There was a small billabong at Gin Downs; I had to toss your sisters in once a day. By Jove, that was a ball—a whole flock of tribal gins and only a few of us. We had to work around the clock to service all of them, as a good cocky would say. The man wiped his wet mouth. "You're going to have a good splash when this pool is finished."

Curly interrupts. "Would we have all of it here, I mean all those things the chaps had up at Gin Downs?"

"Here it's going to be a ritual bath, with *didjeridu* music and

60

chanting; that's how abos mate in the bush." His mouth stays partly open, halfway between a smile and open laughter. "What a pity my old friend Dusty up at the Downs didn't know about that; the poor chap was after pubic hair all the time, but we thought he was only interested in knitting."

I had better move away and let them carry on with the work, whatever good or bad it will bring us. I doubt if the hole will be of any help to our people, not judging by the look on Gunbuna's face. The old man sits on the ground, leaning against a log with his eyes closed, but his lips move now and then and it looks as though . . . yes, he is silently chanting a name.

The whites can still be heard carrying on. "We had such a time when they brought the batch of those noninitiated girls. Bloody fantastic. Good old Dusty, he had to struggle with the lot. That's when he got himself a set of knitting needles," sniggers Redhead.

Gunbuna must be talking to Djanbuwal to urge our ancestor to come with help. The fellows say he chanted silently like that during that boom. I'm not sure how many of these ditches the whites dug then, but there must have been a few of them and that meant that every old man in our country had to chant. The *balandas* did not like the sound of it. More and more of them arrived, and the country looked as though it was being invaded by swarms of grasshoppers; every man carried a *griga* and rucksack while they combed the bush. The whites made big camps west of Mangrove Bay, cut down the tallest trees and stacked the trunks in the sea down near Cape Balanda to make a pathway over the water. Wagudi said that our people thought at first that the whites were going to build a trestle bridge over the narrow strait at the mouth of Mangrove Bay and feared that later on they might stretch it farther out across the sea. The wooden pathway made a jetty and did not bridge the mainland with

61

Bralgu as every tribal soul had at first feared it would. Soon after the boats arrived, bringing piles of corrugated iron sheets to set up camps along the coast. The men with *grigas* moved inland later, chasing every black woman they laid eyes on. My *momo*, a young girl then, saw it all.

"I'd like to get to Gin Downs. The place sounds great," says Curly.

"I doubt there's much of it there now. My old friend Dusty died—lightning struck the bugger. What a pity, bags of hair gathered and not even a knitted tea cosy to show for it."

Luckily Djanbuwal rushed in to help. The elders say that the *balandas* were a tough lot, and they put up quite a fight. They brought in their airplanes and all those machines that the whites are mad on, and morning after morning they swoop over the mainland to chase our spirits out to the sea and farther on to Bralgu. The *balandas* say that it was someone else they were after, but who else would fight in Galwan country but the black man and his spirits.

"It would've been the end of the abos during the boom if the old doc hadn't rushed in with the Bible. What a fool!" Redhead carries on loudly.

Whatever the whites may have brought with them, Djanbuwal had the final say. On the shore of Mangrove Bay, where the waves fall back at low tide, a wreck appeared on the surface and in the soft evening sun it looked like the carcass of an enormous porpoise that the angry sea has brought out to the edge of the water. Inland from the bay, on the fringe of the mangrove forest, there is an airplane; only the tail end can be seen sticking out of the ground like a spear. West of Djangau Peninsula, across the bay from Mount Wawalag and farther down inland lie hills of sooty rocks and plains of dead trees. There are many split boulders there, too. It is from the blasting, many say, but my *momo* thinks our sky ancestor, Djanbuwal, did it striking from the clouds with his mighty *larban*, the "lightning spear," to chase the whites.

" 'Jesus Christ has sent me to witness this,' " cried the old doc during the boom. He's the boongs' friend, you know, wants them to breed instead of perish."

Some people say when he saw what was happening to our people, Cross went to plead to his boss, that Jesus or Justice Man. However, I like to think it was Djanbuwal who saved us, not a *balanda*.

"This idea of doc's better work. With this new mining boom, the boongs'll have to breed mighty quick to catch up with all those losses."

"When'll you be off to that mining place in the bush—the new job, I mean?" Curly asks.

"I hope to leave in a week. It's quite a place they're building up at the uranium province."

"Deep in the reserve, I gather? Would there be many gins?"

"There should be some. Look, sonny, I'll try to get you a job there. What about that, hey?"

With the boom over, the whites gathered their tools in haste and fled from Galwan to their own country to lick their wounds; all but one man—Dr. Cross. From the bay he traveled toward the rising sun, made his way into the bush across the neck of the peninsula, down Gunga River and, just at its end, where the fresh water fell into the sea, he climbed up the cliff. He dragged in some corrugated iron sheets and put up his own hut with a cross on top sticking up toward the sky. Both Gunbuna and his brother, Marngit, were there to help him with it. He showed them a piece of paper, claiming it had come from his boss. The paper read: ". . . No white man shall tread on the reserve unduly, nor should black man raise his spear in anger."

"Does the old doc know you will be working for his son?"

"The two men are friendly. Actually, his son must be glad the old man got those abos locked in here. It's much easier to fiddle with gins than dig ditches or mess up water holes." While he was laying out the last sheet of green plastic a clump of earth fell on Redhead's lip; he was going to brush it off but spat instead.

CHAPTER SEVEN

Fronds of the marin palm sway, the leaves of bushes rustle, lashed by sounds of didjeridu and clapping boomerang from nongaru, the place of virgins; the bush trembles.

The girl rests, cushioned by green branches. A white hand pushes her backward and tucks some greenery under her back. Fair and spotty looks the hand; the fingers slide down diridiri and the thighs stretch.

The skin smeared with malnar drips with sweat; air, branches, grass—everything smells of the sacred color; soon the earth will be saturated with it, too. From nongaru, the tribal mother, the elders sing: "Bugalili, bugalili, bugalili—come to life again!" The calls bounce from the edge of the bush and fly across the country to the spirit world.

The white fingers part maularn, ("lips") and a lizardlike tongue flickers from inside. The skin at the fringe of the vagina is never black and hardly differs in color from white fingers; the tongue looks red like the tongue of a lizard. The people look different, though; the spirits and their worlds do also, but the blood of humans and animals alike always stays red.

Young girls of Cockatoo Tribe penetrated with boomerang
—erect penis longer than Julungul
at sacred walg, the mother of yuln
Bugalili, bugalili—rise to life again!

The tip of the boomerang presses against the dagu *of the girl.*
When pushed aside, the lips change color fast. They might turn
red, black or something else; not woman, but a man only can tell
that.

The red lizard tongue pushed inside refuses to budge any
farther and beats against the tip of the boomerang. The tongue,
warm from inside the womb, strikes against wood again. The
boomerang stays firm, but the white hand holding the wood
quivers.

The girl clenches her teeth; her head swings backward and
sinks farther into the green branches; her mirigin *stick out—*
two bare anthills painted with red ocher piercing the sky.

Bugalili, bugalili . . . !

The white hand twists the boomerang. The red lizard tongue
strikes back, cutting its head against the wooden blade.

The girl whimpers through partly opened teeth.

The whites are staring inside the enclosure; a bearded man
holds a camera to his eye and tracks me with it wherever I go.
With him is a freckle-faced girl, perhaps younger than I, holding a notebook and moving a pencil quickly over the paper—
page after page. They are saying something—the *balandas* want
me to come closer. The girl takes a small packet of sweets from
her bag, unwraps one and shows it to me; it looks like a piece of
biscuit. She chews one and then munches with her lips loudly
to lure me. No, I had better stay away from the fence. I have to
warn the others to keep away from her. A while ago, standing in
front of the camera, she spoke into the microphone: "No man

66

fought harder to save the aborigines than Doctor Cross. During the big mining boom, a generation or so ago, he helped the natives with the Bible. He is helping them again but with much more advanced means—by their genes. The doctor hopes to improve the genetic structure of the tribal blacks, thus making them fit to survive the new industrial boom."

The camera follows me, then it moves on to Gunbuna. The old man has lost his *lap-lap,* and he must look funny to the *balandas* with nothing around his waist; they are giggling loudly. He rests on the sand with both eyes closed and his mouth opening silently now and then. The old man must be talking to his brother Marngit to ask him to plead with our spirits for help. It would not be us he is concerned with; food comes regularly to the enclosure, and there is a large sandpit to dig into overnight. Ure is the one who needs help. No one talks about what has happened to him, but the faces of the elders can tell you as clearly as words when they are worried about someone.

The white girl takes a small mirror and reflects the sun onto Gunbuna's hip. The light tickles the old man's skin, and he thinks it is a fly and tries to brush it off with his hand without opening his eyes. The spot of light moves up his abdomen, dances for a while on the tribal marks on his chest and stops on his wrinkled old face. They want him to get up and walk toward the fence facing the camera; but without looking at the whites, Gunbuna crawls over the ground to hide behind the nearest bush.

The whites have gathered round, a whole mob of them; it must be something special, like our *nara.* There, between the enclosure and the veranda, tables set with food and drink have been brought out and placed under the huge banyan tree. The *balandas* are cleanly dressed, mostly in white; they glance over here while they chat, and now and then they raise their glasses. Doctor Cross is out there too. He sits in a squatter's chair and looks worn out; it is not food or drink but age that has pinned him to the seat. The girl with the notebook is trying to talk him into something. I would rather not stand by the fence, but I will stay nearby in case the whites say something about Ure. Yesterday Wurulu showed me an old water bag. "Which of you had this?" she asked. I said nothing, but she must surely have known that whoever owned it must have headed out into the bush, for there you can drink from water holes and do without the white man's gear.

They help the doctor to sit in the chair. "You are on the verge of making a breakthrough in genetic development, is that right?" asks the girl, while the camera moves in on his face.

"We are endeavoring to produce a new breed. The natives have a unique hybrid property—they have survived for fifty thousand years." The voice reminds me of a fire that has burned down and is almost about to fade into ashes.

"Would they cross with those intelligent samples you selected from our race?"

"A native woman can only conceive in her ritual environment. We have recreated something of that ambience here."

Wurulu still looks inside the enclosure, but she no longer tries to lure me to this fence. Yesterday she told me, "We have all of you in here but that wild young man; the doctor doesn't like any of your lot running astray." Yes, she must have known to whom the water bag had belonged.

The girl with the notebook glances at the enclosure. "How many specimens do you have, Doctor?"

"Only a handful—the natives have become rare now. We got them chiefly from the Galwan bush; this group here is about the lot."

"They're from the uranium province."

A shadow falls on Doctor Cross's face. "Don't confuse people with the stones." The old man might be the same age as Marngit, a bit older perhaps. The two of them called each other *wawa* ("brother"); and being healers, each could seek out pain better than any other man. *Momo* thought that Cross stayed in our country to learn all the sacred words and that once he knows how to chant them the white man will paint his skin and trick our ancestors into doing him a favor. She dared not say anything about it to Marngit, not because she was his sister but because a medicine man can only be told by the spirits whom he should not befriend.

"Will they breed?"

"We've tried for years but mainly with worn-out specimens. We have recently obtained a very healthy one, however, who will surely yield." Doctor Cross had his *dal*, as has any of our medicine men. During the boom he helped Marngit escape from an *ingabunga*, rubbed his wounds with some smelly stuff the whites carry around in a box with a red cross on the top and led him back to Mount Wawalag. "Chant again *wawa*, for your God and mine to hear," he told Marngit.

"Does that mean a virgin birth, Doctor?"

"Not quite. The mating . . ." The doctor's voice fades away suddenly. The nurse calls out for a glass of water and slaps his cheek slightly until he speaks again; ". . . has a ritual context. We provide the perfect environment—an archetypal bush setting . . . will corroborate their spiritual . . . spiritual . . . spiritual . . . ("values," whispered the nurse) . . . it should work."

The doctor has grown old. He never comes inside the enclosure but is often seen walking along the veranda with the help of a stick if Wurulu is not there to lean on. Scores of younger people have long gone, and I wonder why he has not departed too. But . . . perhaps there is nowhere for him to go. Maybe he stayed too long in Galwan country, hunting with our fellows and was invited to take part in our ceremonies. He wanted our fellows to come into his hut in return, to sing about Jesus or Justice, and gave them all a piece of biscuit. The man kept a

69

small case with a red cross painted on it and rushed around when anyone had a spear wound, was suffering from snake bite or cut his toe on a sharp rock. The women giggled whenever they talked about him because when any of them had a child he was always ready to rush in and give a hand. Yes, he helped mother too; he came to help again when she bore me. I doubt whether his Jesus or Justice would have liked it much, and perhaps he does not want him in the spirit world with the rest of the *balandas* and would rather lump him in with us. He could be around for a while yet, I reckon, until the white man's boss and ours sit down together and decide where the old men should go. Perhaps the whites expected Jesus or Justice to call in here today, hoping to have a word with him, but since he did not turn up for such a big gathering, with good food and drink, he must be very far away.

The freckle-faced girl wipes the dust from the plaque, which reads: "DONATED BY THE ADDER CORPORATION." Standing beside it, she turns to the camera. "For the man whose work on the half-caste and quarter-caste breeds is well known, success has come in the sunset of his life. Once, he said to an aboriginal ritual leader, 'Give me your hand, my brother. I will find a home for both of us.' The offspring born at this center will be the first natives to eat with a spoon and live under a roof."

Had Doctor Cross stayed in our country, Marngit could have asked our spirits to make room at Bralgu for his *wawa*, too. I doubt if that will happen now; there are too many of our own souls waiting; and when Ure reaches Mount Wawalag he will have such a long story to tell that our medicine men will have to chant *bugalili* for days and nights if Djanbuwal is to come and free our country again.

They got us to make a big *nara*, not so big as the word says—five men and me, the only woman. Gunbuna did not speak a word,

70

and the others hardly said anything. It is the wrong place to hold the ceremony, and perhaps not the proper time to make it either. Wurulu brought me *dugaruru*; it has split and the piece could fall off at any time. The stone must have been used during the young days of our *momo* by the look of it, and it has a lumpy gray surface. She tries to convince me. "It's very old, a museum exhibit. Take good care of it, won't you." The nurse also brought half a bag of cycad palm nuts; I had better sit down and pound some of them. The stone should be placed on the ground between the knees; the legs have to be kept well apart for the men to see between them, if I am right.

From the open dagu, *down the smeared skin streams blood, it drips to the leaves and shrubs and seeps to the ground, warm as the first monsoon rain.* "*From pierced* dagu, *blood flows into a billabong to quench the thirsty earth. Bugalili, bugalili . . .*

I should have been smeared with red ocher, goanna fat and . . . the blood, too. "Don't be so fussy, the doctor has programmed everything." Wurulu tells me. It sounds as though the *nara* is theirs, not ours.

Without the sight of blood, however, new life will never come—every Galwan girl knows that. One of the Wawalags, the first black woman to become a mother, used her menstrual flow to lure Julungul, the mythical python, from his totemic place. *Momo* said it happened while our ancestral sisters, Balari and Garangal, with their dog, Muru, were journeying through Nilibidi, a stony country in the reserve. The women carried a *badi* ("dilly bag") full of stone blades; one of them had a child . . . yes, it was afterbirth, not menstrual blood, which came when they were sheltering in *murlg* ("bark hut") one stormy night. From a nearby water hole, Julungul watched both women and, as they fell asleep, crawled out and encircled the hut. That night both the Wawalags and their dog were swallowed up, but the following day the snake spat them all out. Not

71

only were the sisters reborn but everything that grows in the black man's country burst into new life—animals, birds and plants as well.

Bugalili, bugalili—come to life again.

The Wawalag story happened at the beginning of our world. Now, whenever *nara* is held, our men sing to tell the story of how the sisters later traveled across the land from sunrise to sunset, naming the places and tribal countries that lie along the coast of the reserve. At the end of their journey the sisters went to Bralgu, and now they appear in the dreams of the tribal elders to tell them how we should hold our ceremonies; *nara*, especially.

"Go on, make the most of it," Wurulu tells us. Wagudi is to play *didjeridu* and the nurse brings him the pipe with Julungul painted on it in colored lines, most of which have faded away. He could only manage a few blows, one at a time, and then gave up. Next to him sits Gunbuna with a pair of *bilma* in his hands. The old man is fairly deaf and does not sing as he should. No, his mouth is not opening at all. Instead someone else is heard; not just one man but a whole group is chanting. The voices sound young and vigorous, just as one would hear them in the bush.

Blood running down from the young girls, like blood from a speared
    kangaroo . . .
Running down among the cabbage palm foliage . . .
Blood that is sacred, running down from the young girl's uterus;
Flowing like water, from the young girls of the coastal tribes . . .

The chant must have come from a transistor or some other white man's machine; the *balandas* have a way of catching the voice and locking it in a small, flat box; then they let it out when they feel like listening to it. The singing does not please Gunbuna; the old man looks as though he has just swallowed a

72

whole anteater; it is one of Narku, *dua* people's songs, but perhaps it is chanted at the wrong time or the way the whole thing is set up must be painful. Gunbuna pretends that he is going to sleep, and his head droops toward his knees, but as soon as he begins to nod the nurse pokes the end of a long rod into his ribs and forces him to spring up. The old man raises both his hands in the air and claps the sticks, directing the noise toward Wurulu and calling, "Bugalili! Bugalili!"

Two men, Dadangu and Gara, are to dance, but they do not make much of it; they move slowly over the patch of sand, burdened with heavy limbs. They look worn-out before they have raised the dust, let alone made the ground tremble. They are supposed to come to me, eat the cycad nuts,to give them strength and then dance about to show their manhood; not much of it is seen now. Each piece of nut, even a fragment, has the blood and life of *djuwei*, "the spirit child waiting to be reborn"; *nara* not only means a ceremony, it is the word for everything that grows: trees, animals and plants, even man. After the festivities, the whole country will burst into new life—human and animal alike. If new children do not come, who will bring the rain in the future, and when the monsoon pours down for months, who will be here to ask our ancestors to get rid of the clouds? Later, when the drought grips the land, the last fish will die in a dried-out claypan and not a single leaf will be left. The whole country will become bare rock where not even a patch of lichen can grow.

Blood, flowing like water . . .
Always there, that blood, in the cabbage palm foliage . . .
Sacred blood flowing in all directions . . .
Like blood from the sacred kangaroo, from the sacred uterus . . .

Let us go and splash in the billabong—I hope that will be all right; the water might help to bring some life to both men, as it

73

does to everything else. They have made my *murlg* ("small hut") just over there on the bank; it is not much, only two corrugated iron sheets put up in an A-shape and with an armful of straw on the ground. I will retire there after the bath and wait for the men . . . I doubt that anyone will come; the cycad nut I pounded is still there. Without it the men have no strength to complete the *nara*, nor will the spirits be lured into bringing new life.

"Hey, come out with me," the nurse calls from the bank of the billabong.

"Should I go to my hut?"

"Leave that; the men are useless!"

"It's the right way to do it; the men should come to my hut!"

"You've had enough fun; that should do it."

We walk toward the building, and halfway to the exit from the enclosure she mutters, "You're making history, Julie. The doctor is so anxious to see the project through; he has grown old, you know.

"Come on, Julie. Let's go inside."

What a pity she has dragged me out of the enclosure. Our men are far too unhappy to be in a ceremonial mood, and the chanting sounds strange. However, I could try to hope that the spirits can be called up. They might despise the bars and the wire, but being black, they have to come to us; just as the monsoon rain returns to the country every year. With a good shower, even the seed scattered over the boulders hardly ever fails to shoot. The tribes grew the same way.

CHAPTER EIGHT

They pumped the water out of the billabong in the hope that *dugaruru* might be lying in the sand at the bottom. I do not remember throwing the stone in, but the whites will not take my word for it and they might even start digging up the ground.

Wurulu is angry. "It couldn't have been taken from the enclosure; even if some of your spooks had been there, there are no holes in the wire for the stone to go through. Even the funnel has mesh over it." They have been after the stone for days, searching under every single bush, turning over logs, shining their torches into every hollow as if they are after a bandicoot that has sneaked into a dark corner to hide.

"It's a precious piece from the doctor's collection; I shouldn't have let it out of my sight."

It sounds as though she blames me, but . . . what use could that stone have been to anyone? You have *dugaruru* of your own; not one that you have found or taken from someone else but the stone that has been part of you . . . before being born, I suppose. Yes, *momo* told me a lot about it.

"I haven't let him know the stone is missing yet—let's hope it turns up."

Before a child is born, *djuwei*, ("spirit") comes from his father country and enters the woman-mother-to-be. With him he brings all the secrets and *marain*, the "sacred side of life"; *dugaruru* comes in that way too, but no one has ever seen the stone entering the body. The spirits have their secretive way of doing that, just as they do when they shape unborn children and give them a face, bones, blood and flesh. *Dugaruru* is given to the girl child so that when she grows up she can give birth to new children. *Momo* thinks that the stone is somewhere deep in the womb and it only comes out now and then to let men make love to us; then it finds its way back again.

"It'll break the doctor's heart; he cherished that wretched stone more than the whole collection," moans the nurse.

"Let's hope it'll turn up." Redhead wades through the billabong; there is only a shallow pool of water left in it.

"This could finish doc off!"

My mother, she bore me, sister Jogu and the others—I am not sure how many. I tried to ask Wagudi the other day; he is sure of Plonk but vague about the others. Whenever we talk about it he tries to count them on his fingers, stutters their names, remembers the color of their skins and the way their hair grew but cannot recall where they have all gone. He has seen them, though he is not sure where. That could only be the truth—old people know that if they say otherwise, they will never be led to Bralgu to join the other spirits. It would have been better if we had all been born in our own country. People are no different from the trees of grass that bursts into life not long after *nara*. They grow and flourish during the Wet, in the days of warm sun and the soft soil that covers the whole countryside; when, as night passes into day and *wanba*, "Morning Star Pigeon," calls to the new dawn to rouse all life, it looks as if everything is striving upward to bridge earth and sky.

"You're not going to tell doc yet, I suppose." Redhead stamps with his bare feet on the wet sand, all that is left of the billabong.

"Not yet . . . we'd better make sure first." Her voice is weakening.

"You never know, it could turn up."

"No, I don't think it's here."

There is an end to every track, and the good season of the year passes away as does anything else. The grass sucks out the last drops of wet, and as the ground turns rock-hard the green stems dry up. They sway in the wind as though making their own dance for rain and chant in the breeze, but the clouds do not come. Only a dry storm rushes in from the far plain across the country to flatten the spear grass and carry the fragments away to an unknown world. Even the trees find it hard to struggle on; most of them lose their leaves, their branches droop and often only the bare trunks are left, looking like poles—they are lucky if they survive at all. As the year goes round, the clouds come, but the rain does not fall again and the whole country shrinks into an ugly desert.

Wurulu's face has grown grim. "I feared this might happen."

"Did doc feel that, too?"

"One of their spooks often visits him at night; it must be Marngit, that witch doctor he told us about."

"Visits, what for?"

"He always chants. We got it on tape once. The doctor translated it later. It said: "We shall turn into trees—a whole forest of us. When you grind the country into dust, our souls will be there, too."

Redhead came out of the billabong and the two walked slowly toward the building. "No spooks ever troubled us when we were at Gin Downs."

"It's a pity that young man has gone on the loose."

"My old boss used to say that one bird doesn't make a flock, in their world or ours."

Wurulu stopped. "They might turn that lad into *marngit* if he reaches his tribal country. He'll excite those simple souls. The whole tribe'll be destroyed; the doctor fears that might really happen."

"That young boong'll be trapped all right—hardly any of them have made it across the reserve."

The whites pass the bush I am hiding behind, and as they walk off their voices die away. I can no longer hear the words, but I sense that Ure, as much as *dugaruru*, will be on their minds for a long time.

The desert apple is a strange shape; it looks as if the tree has shrunk to the size of a bush with its stunted branches against the sky; most of the leaves have fallen—drought or wind might have something to do with that—and only the crop remains clinging to the bare branches; I do not think I have seen a tree like this before. The fruit is fleshless—nothing but solid nuts, rock-hard, that split in two in the heat of the sun. Someone should tell Gunbuna; the old man has been hanging round the tree all day. He has gathered a heap of fruit, but there is nothing to pound them with; he chews one and if he tries to crack it, the nut could break his jaw.

There has been no food for days. Perhaps the whites are waiting for us to come up with the lost stone before we are given any tucker. Through the mesh shutter at the end of the enclosure we can see a dead wallaby lying on a trolley in the supply room; it has been there for a while because blowflies are buzzing round it merrily, but Redhead is resting in a chair and is in no hurry to chuck the carcass through the shutter. I had better stand here and stare at the food. The whites do not like you hanging about, and they might give us the wallaby, not because we are hungry but just to brush me off. Doctor Cross will see me, too; he is in front of Redhead looking out of TV box. I can see every single hair of his head and . . . he is smiling at me.

"They have bred ritually ever since they have been on this continent . . ."

" . . . but always in the bush, of course." It is the girl with the notebook again, but somehow it is only her voice coming from TV box.

"We use their customs as ethnic stimuli and decoy the human body into conceiving."

"Doctor, are you sure that she has conceived?"

"We provided them with their traditional environment—experimentally of course—whereas they would normally mate according to tribal rituals."

"Doctor, what if a child is born outside his tribal area?"

"He won't belong to the tribal country. Only those born there can have full ritual status."

The girl's voice is heard again. "Who coordinates the fertility rites?"

"The medicine man, normally."

"How did you crack the breeding code?"

"I'm related to one of them, in a manner of speaking. The man took me as his brother. That was a long time ago, but the native still calls to see me now and then."

The screen darkens for a moment while the sound of *did-jeridu* rises and voices call "Bugalili! Bugalili! . . ."

The freckle-faced girl coughs. "Doctor, just how important are these rituals to the mating process?"

"They are believed to invoke the spirits from the totemic place of the tribal country. The process is rather primitive, but you have to know the right call to get the women to conceive."

Sacred girls of Cockatoo Tribe pierced by boomerang
—erect penis longer than Julungul
the sacred womb—place of yuln, stuffed with semen.

79

"How long is the mating season?"

"About the same time as us, I presume. The litter might be somewhat later because of her being confined in the enclosure."

"In one of your papers, Doctor, you stressed that breeding like this is essential if the aborigines are to survive."

The doctor leaned forward. "We are here to improve the genetic endowment of mankind."

"Your sperm bank is exclusively from donors with outstanding IQs?"

"Yes. Those primitives have lived for fifty thousand years; the stock needs genetic improvement."

"Will this project mark the end of your lifelong endeavors for the blacks?"

Something has happened. The doctor's face has changed into a claypan caught in the heat of the day; the edges of it dry out quickly, and before you can blink it becomes a hardened crust. Then, as the sun sucks out the last of the remaining moisture from the depths of the shattered surface, the earth changes into rocklike lumps. A sound is heard too—not that of man, animal or insect but of stones falling. Even the light seems weak, as though it is about to fade away forever.

No man is seen or heard; the enclosure looks hollow now, an empty trap. Over the metal structure booms the sound of bells.

Wuluru appears from inside the building. "Come here, Julie." Her voice hardly says much and as she lets me pass through the doorway, she spins in her hand a small yellow cross suspended on a tiny chain. It seems as though nothing much has happened, either in her world or in mine.

Where are the men? I should ask her. Waking up some moments ago, I found the enclosure deserted; I went around poking my toes into the ashes of the fire but felt hardly any warmth. The men must have been taken away at dawn.

The bells toll. From inside the building they sound like the roaring of an immense beast.

"Every soul is stricken by grief." The tiny chain stops swaying; she holds two ends of it above the back of her neck. "Clip them together for me."

What has happened to the *balandas*; have they left, too?

The bells toll. Has the world come to an end, white men's and ours?

"He was such a great man; his soul will be welcomed in both worlds."

Our *marngit* will be able to tell whether he was great or not; Gunbuna might know that, too. "What have you done to our fellows?"

"They're all out to see off the boss."

I had never seen her veiled before; she is wearing a long dress, for the ceremony perhaps. She looks much nicer without her white uniform. "Plonk—he'll be going there, too?"

"I thought you might fancy him." She glanced out through the window.

I like her much more talking like this and not fiddling around me with her medical instruments and asking questions as she always did before. With Doctor Cross gone, she might never wear that white overcoat again. So much the better.

"I got him into decent clothes. Come here and see him; they say 'garb maketh the man.' "

Outside Redhead leads our men into his Land Rover. Instead of lap-laps around their waists each of the fellows wears a red cloth. Plonk looks different, though.

"Julie, I doubt you'll be seeing much of him. It's going to be beyond our control now."

Poor Plonk—he looks so strange in white man's clothes. Doctor Cross was twice his size, the sleeves of the white shirt

81

have swallowed both his arms; a pair of shorts, though held by braces, hang down halfway between his knees and his feet; a red tie matches his canvas hat.

"The whole town will attend the service. The doctor's son should be there, too. We expect him to call here also; he might take control of the place."

The bells toll. Redhead slams the car door after his passengers and takes his seat behind the steering wheel.

Wuluru holds a pair of gloves but hesitates to put them on. "I'm still after that lost stone. Would you have one of your own?"

"Every black woman has one."

"Where do you hide yours?"

"Up in the bush, at the rubbish dump."

"If I let you out, would you take long to get it?"

"It's about half a camp walk."

"Take your time."

I wonder if Muru is still at the old camp. When they are alone, animals stay for a while and then wander off to someone else. The dog might be heading toward Galwan. Perhaps there is a shortcut through the bush known only to animals, spirits and stars that humans never find. It is not that they should not know, but if the blacks learn it the whites will follow them and find out how to reach the tribal country wihout having to struggle through the bush. Maybe it is better this way. Then neither spirits nor stars nor animals will tell a single word, and it would be hard to follow any of them.

She hands me a paper bag. "Take some sandwiches, some oranges too. You'll have a long walk."

She must know I am not coming back and says: "I hope Muru, your dog, hunts well."

"Like us, dingos seldom go hungry in the bush."

"I told you of that friend of mine, he would not part with his

82

for the whole world."

"Was he black or white?"

"It's soul that matters, not the skin, so they say."

Wuluru opens the door to let me out. "We all make mistakes, Julie. A mistake brought us to this world, according to the Bible."

The bells toll. I have to hurry and get out while the town mourns. Ranger and Plonk will be at the church; they too would be stricken with grief, though I doubt they will say a word to each other.

PART
TWO

CHAPTER ONE

The river has weakened, but is now as clear as drops of morning dew, and it chatters as it cascades over the rocks.

Here you do not have to look into the pools and search for floating leaves, straw or twigs to find out which way the river is flowing, if at all. The water finds its way through gaps in the boulders and is channeled out of the gorge in a rushing stream, weaving honeycomb patterns on the surface as it slides down, nudged by the hard hips of the rocks. Then, as it comes out of the pass, the water, almost at the end of its strength, sighs and fans out into a shallow pool, showing how much of it there really is. The blurred sky is mirrored in the water; the air is laden with haze. There must be a fire somewhere around.

You do not often see the river at its best; perhaps once, in the right season, on a calm day, or sometime in your early life. Then as you grow up, stumbling through a different world, you hear the murmur of the cascade and see it once again, but only in a dream. The sight or sound of it—perhaps both—makes man search for that magic again sooner or later.

How far have I gone? Hardly a handful of camps. I have to

keep counting the days on my fingers . . . and on my toes as well. Some nights ago, *momo* visited my dreams. She thinks that there are more camps from here to our country than all the Galwan people together could count. She must be right, for once a soul journeys across the reserve the memory lingers, even in old age.

Is that smoke I smell—it is hard to tell. With it comes a sound, faint and distant. Could it be a man or an animal, the howling of the wind perhaps.

Trees must feel the same as humans: they flock around the river, plunge their roots into the cracks of the rocks or into an occasional patch of soil. Although the soil is as hard as rocks, the plants grip it and hold on, glad to see the shadow of the dancing leaves tickling the smooth face of the water.

A noise floats through the air, not the wind or an animal cry but a whirring metallic sound. It must be coming from the plain down below the gorge. It is a worn-out sound that matches the murmur of the cascading water and echoes against the rocks. Yet it hovers about like an intruding insect that has sneaked inside the gorge and is trapped between the bluffs. It is a machine, I reckon; the *balandas* never travel in the bush without one. I hope they are not after me. So many days have passed since I left town that I should have been forgotten by now. Perhaps it is not the whites who are tracking me but animals. Perhaps the whites are even searching for rocks, chipping off pieces here and there and putting them into knapsacks the way Ranger used to do.

The haze grows thicker. Where is all this smoke pouring in from? There is a shady spot behind that bluff, and if I sweep away some of the small stones before stretching on the ground the rest will do my poor legs some good. On the rocks above, the green scrub partly shelters the ground down below. It will be hard to see much of this place from the sky, but the whites might be hunting some of us. They are a noisy lot when they are traveling in the bush with their machines. "You can tell a metal beast either by the sound or the smell," Ure said. When they are in the bush, the *balandas* make noises to frighten off our spirits. The machines can track men just as well as dogs. I wonder how it can do this when it flies so high.

The sound of the machine must have hit the stone walls opposite the river head-on and bounced back down the gorge. I doubt that they will get the man they are after, however good their machine is at tracking. Yesterday, down the river, I passed the place where the poor fellow had camped—a small rock shelter at the base of a bluff. He must have been here days ago. There is some dried-out heart of cabbage palm on the ground that might have been there for a whole moon. It is a pity the country here is so rocky. A footprint on the ground could tell me which tribe he came from, how fast he is traveling and if he is hungry. He must have known that the whites would be about, for when you are hunted you do not make a fire; you would rather chew the palm raw than let the smoke give you away.

The rattling sound fades away; it is hard to tell which way it has gone. Whoever it might have been—the *balandas* or their spirits—they must have grown tired of the bush and turned back to their home. I had better press on up the river and watch my step. If I keep to the rocks I will leave no footprints. Moving around the water pools, I have to stay away from soft, sandy ground that gives away man and animal alike. A smoky haze has blurred the air; a smell of burning scrub lingers, too. The whites like to strike matches whenever they are out in the bush. "That lot are dead scared of the trees," *momo* often told me. Too blind to see smoke, she sensed it better than any of us and always felt wary, just as reptiles do.

I was never told how *momo* became blind. It must have happened when she was young, and it had to do with whites.

High above circles a small flock of crows with cries in their beaks. The smoke has excited the scavengers.

Even if he is blind, in the bush a man can tell his own country. Trees know you; the birds, too. I often had to take *momo* around, always walking in front of her with a rod between us. A forward stroke meant to walk faster; a turn of the stick to the right told me to look for shade, and the same movement to the left, well . . . I have forgotten what that was for. She was taken to Mount Wawalag to see her brother Marngit. That was long before I was born, and ever since, *baba* has kept saying, "No healer can help you to see if both eyes have gone." However, our medicine man helped her, not to see, but to hear trees. Marngit must have told every soul in the bush to talk to her in their strange lingo. She even knew whether there were clouds on the Wawalag peaks, although the mountain and the sky above were half a country away from us. She could sense when Ranger was around as well. Say nothing, just sigh, and the leading rod would usually spin for us to lead her out of the way quickly.

The scavengers can smell burning reptiles about a half a horizon away, so my *momo* says. Would Ure have passed by Gin Downs? I wonder.

A clump of cabbage palms grows around the edge of a large slab, hardly a shade away from the river. The place, shielded from the outside by foliage, lets the sun break in only here and there, leaving fishbone patterns on the boulder. Our fellows must have come here often to sharpen *gara* ("flint") for their spears and stone axes. The grooves in the slab look deep; some of them have already been overgrown with lichen or are partly buried in silt. Look! Someone has been here lately to file his tools. No, I doubt if that mark would have been made by a spear; the groove is too shallow, and it has been grooved into the slab. A few drops of blood have been left behind, too. Ure should

90

have wiped them off. There are no pieces of metal to be seen; he must have tossed the handcuffs into the river and, feeling victorious at getting rid of them, forgot to throw some dirt into the freshly made groove in the rock. Ure should be wise enough to keep away from Gin Downs.

Farther upstream the river gorge has narrowed with bluffs rising up to the sun from the edge of the water. The rocks in the stream look smooth; you would not be able to hold on to the wet, slippery surface with your feet. Toes lose their hold easily and slide down; even if you used our hands and tried to move forward, your fingers would fail to grip and your helpless body would splash into the water. I should look for a bit of shade to rest in and then walk up behind the cliffs to bypass the gorge. Ure must have gone that way, too. He could be near Galwan country, if he is not already there. Will Bungul ask about me? The two brothers will talk about everything that has happened to us in the white man's world—about me as well. What a pity I did not tell Ure I was heading back that way, too; he might need to know that Ranger has his eye on our country again. Bungul will not like that, but he might have already been told by Marngit what the white man is up to. The spirits will know that much better than any of us.

Smoke still blurs the air, and the sky showing in the pool looks leaden, too. There must be a bush fire raging through the hills beyond the bluff. Perhaps it will come this way. I hope that Ranger will not make any fires if he goes back to our country again; no black man or spirit likes to see his home shrouded in ash.

Only the spirits can tell when each of us is to be born and will die, *momo* taught me. I often took her up Gunga Valley, and we always camped at Pandanus Springs halfway upstream, where the river flanks Mount Wawalag from the south. She knew each step of the journey and would stop every now and then to look at a trunk of an old gum tree. "A few branches must have dried up lately." The trees have a lingo of their own to tell humans how they feel, but I was too young then to know much about it. Why did she have so many scars on her thighs and belly?

The smoke has thickened; I can almost feel it in my mouth now. In the bush, set alight during that big boom, even the crocodiles were turned into ashes, not being able to reach the safety of deep water. So *momo* says.

I was told to take her no farther than Pandanus Springs. From there the valley narrows into a gap and Gunga makes a cascading noise as the water rushes down over the boulders. "Why can't we walk farther up?" I asked, and was told that the place was *marain*. Beyond the bluff lies a large billabong. Two rivers run out of it: west flows Malgu into Mangrove Bay and east flows Gunga toward the open sea and the morning sun. The billabong never dries up, not so much because it is in the shade of the mountain but because of the Wawalags sitting on the summit. The sisters urinate often, and the water seeps through the rocks and springs out farther down to form the river.

From Pandanus Springs, the sisters are best seen in the evening when the setting sun spreads a mellow light over their breasts. The skin looks as if it has been smeared with red ocher, as though they are made up ready to come down to the billabong for an initiation ceremony. One of them, Balari, has long, wet hair falling down her shoulders. "Why has she got such big breasts?" I asked.

"To feed all our children."

The other sister, Garangal, has a large belly, a whole boulder of it, and stood on the summit, perpetually pregnant, showing it to every soul in the country. "*Momo*, when shall I be allowed to go to the billabong?"

"As soon as you are ready to be *bala* ["initiated"]."

"What will happen then?"

Momo sat in the shade to rest for a while. She had no diridiri but scar-wrinkled skin instead. "You'll go to goanna country and live with your duwei, ["husband"]." When she was talking about the tribes, she always referred to them by the name of their totem.

I hardly knew my duwei, Bungul, though I used to play with his brother, Ure, whenever I was in Narku country. I had to be Ji, mother of the Wawalags, and he was Boma-Boma, the man trying to force dugaruru from inside me. "Will it hurt when I sleep with Bungul?"

Momo turned her face toward the mountain peaks. "There would not be any tribal people otherwise. The sisters told us so. Don't ever make them angry." I always looked on her as my real mother, whom I had seldom seen. It was not a big age difference between them, a few years at the most.

"Is that why I have to grow up?"

"All of us go through it—fish, birds, every living soul has to bring up its young. Only the rocks are different."

From the bluff over the gorge not much of the country can be seen. The bush is shrouded with smoke, and as it spreads fast it chokes trees and hills, and even the horizon is clotted by the misty mass. Patches of red appear now and then to mark the crown of a tree that has just burst into flames. As the flare subsides, the glowing skeleton of the branches shows for a while before they too are swallowed by smoke. Poor country; it struggles like a mortally wounded reptile.

I can hear the metallic sound again, loud and rattling. With it comes a machine—a huge monster hovering in the air. A snapped-off branch flies from the top of a tree and tumbles through the air, nipped off by the whistling wind. Two men are riding in the metal beast. One of them looks like Plonk! Yes, it must be him—I can see his side-turned mouth, wide open. The

93

canvas hat and that clumsy white shirt—what a fool!

From the gray belly of the machine hangs a long rope with a metal object the size of a fist swaying on the end, almost touching the tops of the trees. It looks like a snake held by the tail while being carried away by a huge bird. Yes, I have heard fellows talking about this in the camp; it is called a helicopter, and it often flies over the reserve. Ure thinks that the thing hanging down from the machine is there to tell the *balandas* all they want to know about rocks. He might be wrong. I reckon it is a python, not a gadget; the whites must have tied something heavy to its head so that the body is stretched down to the ground and . . . who knows more about rocks than snakes. To make the reptile talk the whites have burned the bush, for when they are terrified, man and beast are forced to tell the truth.

The helicopter flies over, following the line of the ridge that extends along the river, then disappears over the plain stretching farther away, toward the haze of the fading sun. No, the men could not have spotted me; I dashed for cover in time and lay still behind a rock the same color as my skin. In the bush the *balandas* see only what they are out to loot; Ranger was like that. I saw him once at Pandanus Springs sneaking down through the gap from the billabong. He stopped for a while to knock pieces of rock off a cliff and tucked them into his rucksack. I said nothing to *momo*.

The sun has been drowned in smoke and I doubt that the helicopter will be back—not today. The *balandas* might be back at their camp already, reaching for a bottle to quench their thirst. Why drag Plonk along? If they hoped to be shown the right track for the machine to follow, they could have been stuck here forever. That fool has never been out in the bush; he could not tell one tree from another and knows nothing about rocks or tracking either.

CHAPTER TWO

Muru has come back.

I slept heavily during the night. After a day-long journey it is hard to wake up, even if you hear whining noises and feel something clawing at your shoulder. I might have shouted at the poor dog or kicked it off. The animal would be just as hurt as humans are after such a long journey not to be welcomed by a single pat.

Muru now lies curled on the ground between me and the fire, part of his body resting against my arm, perhaps to make sure that when I get up I will not slip away and leave him behind. The dog growls, but not at me. Two of his legs move and beneath his skin the muscles are tense and hard; his snout twitches and the whole jaw is trembling. A whole pack of mongrels must be after him or perhaps he ran into a trap that the whites set in the bush. It is an awful dream; I had better wake him up, poor soul.

I dream, too. The night before last Wurulu came to see me, bringing a plastic sheet and a blanket. "Galwan women always have a mat at hand; this should do you instead." There was no anger in her voice. Perhaps she thinks that I am going to become a mother and should have white man's rags to lie on? Why does she bother? In the bush each tribal woman knows when she is pregnant and how to care for a child once it comes. My mother had me on bare sand under that whistling tree, and they wrapped me in soft paperbark to keep me warm. Wurulu came again that same night; tiptoeing around with a brush in her hand she traced a large IQ on my belly. Perhaps that was the name of a child she hoped would come. How could there be one? The chanting was wrong, and Gunbuna had no strength to blow *didjeridu*. Even if the proper sound was heard, the spirits would hesitate to come to the metal enclosure for fear of being trapped. The spirits bring *djuwei*, the "soul of a child," no bigger than a sandfly, and place it in your *walg*, to be mothered there. We all grew from a tiny speck like that, as invisible as the spirits often are. No men but *marngit* are given power to see them.

Tiny as they are, *djuwei* know not to leave the womb until they grow into a human shape. When they do come out they cry and gurgle, for the spirits only give them the power to talk after they have forgotten all about the world they have left so they will not give away its secrets. I have been shown the *djumala*—a large tree on the seashore at Warngi Inlet, hardly a camp walk from Red Cliff where the Gunga River enters if you follow the coastline farther north. The Wawalag sisters can be seen from there, too. In the morning they look half awake when the early sun washes them with red, splashing the sacred color over the mountain bluffs and the slopes below. "No black child is ever born without the sisters seeing," I was told. Not only is the place good for us but the turtles come there to lay their clutches at the right time of the year.

The whistling tree grows huge, elbowing its branches out and up toward the sky, and when a good year comes it drops a heavy crop of cones and spines. What a tree. From a few voices away it seemed as if a cloud, tired of wandering around, has settled down to rest on the soft sand between the dunes and the edge of the beach where the sea rolls in to smooth the land. The water has formed an inlet at that part of the coast that looks like a damper someone has taken a bite out of. They say that a long time ago, Warngi, the sea monster with jaws as big as waves, rode on the storm to snatch the Wawalags away but fell short of the summit and instead bit a good chunk out of the plain below. During the Wet the water floods the plain; it runs down from the hills and rolls in from the sea as well. "None of us come here then?" I asked *momo*.

"During the monsoon women do not bear."

"Why do the sisters watch, then?"

"Ducks—flocks of them come. Ji was one of them."

I liked *momo* telling me about Ji, the Duck Woman, who was seduced by Boma-Boma to whom she was *mugul*, a kind of "niece." That happened in the Dreaming, at the beginning of the world when the country looked dusty and flat without any rocks. There were a few trees but no cycad palms to gather nuts from. There were no customs or girls' initiation ceremonies yet; not till Boma-Boma forced the stone out of Ji's *walg* and the Wawalags came to bear the tribal children. While they are growing up, the young all play *wogal-dua*, the story of Duck Woman, just as Ure and I did, and every young tribal soul is thrilled with the game that is part of our beginnings.

About a shade from the tree where I was born and on the other side of the sand bank is a lagoon, hardly a voice long and a stone's throw wide, one of many around here. During the Wet, water rushes in from the sloping plain below the mountains and keeps the lagoons full for a good part of the year; then during the Dry the level goes down and the water falls as low as . . . hardly up to my knees. The fish are trapped and you can catch eels, turtles and crabs just by walking in.

97

Around the lagoons grow tall paperbarks that often thrust part of their trunks across the shady green pools below, so that their branches are mirrored and their leaves tickle the sleeping face of the water. As the pools shrink after the Wet, vines and bushes follow hungrily, grabbing every bit of exposed ground where they can plunge new roots. Now and then the wind sends swarms of white blossom floating in the air; they come down on the dark green limpid surface and drift slowly to the edges of the pool.

Once I found a duck there, tangled in the vines. At first I could not see the bird; then I heard a rustling in the leaves, so I threw a stone at the sound.

"It's Ji! Let her go, she has brought more young into the world than all those leaves you can see."

"The bird is dead."

Momo's face hardened. "How dare you kill her!"

"I didn't mean to!"

"Your mother never did anything like that."

"Where is she, my mother?" I hardly remembered ever seeing her except in dreams.

Momo held her breath for a moment. "She was sent off by boat; *balanda* man Cross wanted it that way."

"Will she come back?"

"Our women always come back, just as the turtles return to nest here."

For a moment I thought I saw mother under the whistling tree laying a clutch of eggs and asked, "Will she be here before the Dry ends?"

"It's a long journey, only a few of us ever made it."

In her *dua* Narku country, the people often told the story of how once *balandas* raided *nongaru* ground at the billabong and took away a group of young girls who were being initiated. Not many came back; *momo* did, and a few others who suffered

98

hardly less. Old man Gunbuna knew more about that than any other tribal elder; he often paints the story on sheets of bark that he shows around. They say no black soul could stay away from the tribal country forever, and most of the girls reached Narku country finally. Changed into cockatoos and ducks, they fly around, shying away from humans. In the painting they always appear in flocks, just as they do in life, chatting loudly about all they have gone through.

My younger sister Jogu asked me once if mother would come back in a flock or fly in on her own. I could not tell her anything except that far beyond the horizon there is a race of white-skinned people with a lingo very different from ours. When taken there, even if you turn into a flying fox, the journey back will be long and hard.

"Shouldn't our men go and fetch mother?"

Momo kept silent for a while, facing the sea. "She might come by boat . . ."

No one knew when the boat, the barge, the whites named it, would call except Ranger and Doctor Cross. It came during the Dry, often twice, and always anchored against the Red Cliffs above where the Gunga River enters the sea. Whenever it turned up, the Galwan men had to go and unload the boxes and bags from the barge's belly and drag them up the cliffs to the white man's hut set on the top. We never learned what was in them; *momo* thought they were full of barley sugar, red cloth and small mirrors; others guessed they could be boxes of biscuits and bags of tea; but there were some steel axes, for sure. However, only the men who went to Doctor Cross's hut for two whole seasons got one. My father was lucky. Once he brought me a small bag made of shiny colored paper that crackled when you folded it. It had a strong smell of . . . I found bits of tobacco in the bottom. It was empty, yet somehow it looked nice.

I had better slow down and look for some shade. It is the middle of the day and the sun is resting on the top of my head like a burning log. Muru finds the heat hard to take, too. The dog splashes into the water now and then to cool off, and that helps a little. There is no breeze, and the gorge is like a sandpit in full sun. It looks . . . yes, the flanks of the gorge have narrowed to a gap filled with deep water. I passsed a place like that before, downriver. I will have to climb up the bluff again and then follow the ridge to get over the barrier.

There is good shade at the foot of the wall. I'll have a long rest before starting to climb. I must not forget to dip Muru into the water before we leave. The ground is a bit too rough to lie on; I'll sit and lean my back against the rock. There is a draught coming from somewhere. Yes, there is a passage going under a large slab and disappearing behind the rocks. A path leads inside; you can trace it by the worn surface. Perhaps the animals shelter there during the Wet or on cold nights, or to hide from the heat. Muru must have sensed something because he runs inside, then rushes back whining and clawing my arm. Maybe there is a hurt animal in there or . . . perhaps there is a passage from the ridge so that you can come out of the ground far above the gorge. Animals know how to move about far better than humans.

The rocks are partly covered with soot, but it does not look so dark inside. A large opening in one of the walls lets in the daylight; even the sun finds a way in, throwing the shape of the large gap through which it has come onto one wall. The cave looks a good shelter . . . no! On the dusty ground near the entrance, partly sunk in dust, lies a woman's waist belt made of human hair and cockatoo feathers. Near it are several empty cartridges. The metal has long lost its shine and is covered with green spots. Two skeletons are resting up against the wall. Each has a chain attached to a wrist and the metal, long gone reddish in color, has been rubbed against the rocks leaving marks . . .

100

and . . . one link has been half filed off, but something must have run out, either time or human strength. Another skeleton, a smaller one of a woman, lies beside the dead fire, bits of long hair trailing through the ashes. Her face must have been stamped into the fire. The jaws are wide open and look as though they are chewing lumps of charcoal. A step away, a young woman hugs her child. A patch of sun falls on the bones of a tiny hand stretching toward the mother's breast, lights it up for a moment, and then the shadows return. Not far from the fire, one of the women must have lifted a stick but fallen before she had time to swing it. Above her, a dog with a large hole in its head is caught among the rocks. Something unknown, perhaps a dying yell, must have tossed the animal against the cave wall.

In Galwan, the bones of the dead are gathered in a hollow log before they are taken to a burial cave on Mount Wawalag. These remains should be cared for too; they are all black souls. Ure might be back with the other tribal men and . . . yes, he has been here and left his footprints in the dust; he must have forgotten to watch where he stepped. He sat on that boulder for a while and he left his spear thrower behind. I doubt if he wanted to keep it any longer; the whites can have that piece of pipe back, and anything else made of plastic or steel. Ure will make one of wood and feel much happier that the tool comes from the bush and was not molded by the whites.

The sun has slipped behind the cliff, leaving a misty haze in the cave while the darkness creeps from the corners behind the rocks. Two of the skulls can still be seen but, half hidden in the shadow, they too are fast sinking into the dark.

In Galwan I often wondered why birds always perch on the highest trees and eagles nest on the top of crags. Yet however hard man has tried to squeeze himself in among the rocks he has found no safety. Here, so many camps away from town that I cannot keep count, where a horse, beast or machine could hardly find its way, the white man has left his wrath. It is not for land, for there is hardly a patch of it to be seen among the rocks that would be of any use to the *balandas*; no stones have been chipped away either. It could be nothing else but malice or a curse; not that of a man alone but of a god who tells him to hunt for prey.

CHAPTER THREE

Beyond the gorge the country opens out into a wide valley, an immense claypan shaped by our spirit ancestors in the Dreaming, in the time before the trees or birds came to life. It slopes slowly away from the distant flanks of the mountains, boulders showing here and there as they reach above the tall spear grass like reared-up kangaroos on the lookout. Along the bottom of the valley lies a dark green belt that looks like a long snake stretched across the country, its head far away toward the horizon, tucked into the armpit of the distant hills.

A flock of galahs, red-breasted cockatoos, floats in the air above the dry plain and lands on a stunted tree. So many of them! The birds struggle for perches, pushing each other off the crowded branches. What a noisy lot! Not so shy as they are in Galwan. They think that I have come to join them and screech to tell me everything that happened at Gin Downs. "Cockatoos live longer than humans," I was told. If *momo* is here she would know each of them, though they look different now.

Keep on, Muru! A hot day like this wears us out fast. Those boulders are too hot to lean on; we have to keep walking until we find some shade, my furry friend. The river has looped off to the other end of the valley. Look, there is a cluster of trees floating in the heat haze ahead. We have to hold on till we get there. The galahs would like a cool place to rest, too; they are up in the air again, swooping above—more of them than I can count. There should be as many birds above as there are rocks on the ground. The bodies of the girls were turned into boulders, while the spirit of each took to the air to become a bird. The pink feathers tell us that they were coated with red ocher before they were taken away from *nongaru*, the "ceremonial ground." Though the girls have shrunk into fluffy balls, they have not lost the strength of their voices. Poor souls; why have our fellows not come to fetch them? *Momo* often said that young girls are *marain* and no tribal man could be happy to see them taken away. Her brother Marngit should have organized a search party; maybe he did, but Gin Downs was too far to reach? I saw the medicine man when I rested in the shade earlier today and dozed off. He was talking to Ure again. "Keep along the Milky Way, that track leads to our world!" The old man held a boomerang, pointing it toward the horizon. I could not gather whether Ure was being told to travel to Bralgu or Galwan, but wherever he was sent the journey should be safe if the spirits are there to care for you.

Muru is lagging behind again; I should walk more slowly, the heat is hard on the poor soul. That cluster of trees is farther than I thought, and it looks too green and shady even though it is still a good way off. A willy-willy travels across the plain; the wind spins a bundle of weeds high into the air and heads up the valley. It comes to the trees, lingers for a while and then, skirting the grove, hurries toward the horizon. How long does it take wind or spirits to reach Galwan country from here? The journey might wear them out too, though it is much longer for humans. We have to camp and look for water. Those distant hills are so bare. It looks as though the earth, an immense beast, had an aching belly and has thrown out everything from inside her guts. It will be days before I reach them, perhaps more than you can count on the fingers of one hand. The river might end there; then beyond those hills there may be a plain, perhaps made by the spirits for another tribe. Then farther on, another valley where those mighty people from the Dreaming passed; and beyond it again, a chain of mountainlike distant clouds from which the morning star rises, carrying a message from the spirit world to tell the people that they are not forgotten. Somewhere in the mountains there—or is it before there?—there should be a hill called Nagambi with flints for making a good *gara* ("stone spearheads"); every hunter has heard of it. Farther on, there is a paperbark swamp given by the ancestors not only to humans but to birds, crocodiles . . . and the place where Djanbuwal, Thunder Man, keeps all his water. That is not the end; you have to walk much farther toward the morning sun and make many more camps, but the country narrows and the rivers appear smaller, as though there is less land for them to wind through. At last comes Mount Wawalag, sitting on the Djangau Peninsula like the tip of a finger, to mark the end of the land.

The galahs swooped over the valley screeching; something has surely upset them. Shouldn't the dog have sensed someone about?

When I was in Galwan I was told that in the Dreaming our country looked much bigger. The land extended beyond the peninsula, and you could walk across to Bralgu—now many skies away across the sea. "Warngi, he put an end to it." *Momo* told me about the immense sea monster that ate the bridge to our spirit world, and with our ancestors cut off it turned on the mainland. The lower part of the country, with soft soil and sand, was easy to bite off, and he munched it like a hungry man does a damper. Mount Wawalag could have been eaten. A

105

whole land and every black man would have gone if it had not been for one of our mighty ancestors. I think . . . yes, it must have been Boma-Boma. He paved a path across the sky and reaching Bralgu called our spirits to come and chase the monster.

The galahs are here again; the flock sounds louder now, and the birds swoop hardly a spear above me. One of the cockatoos has lost her feathers and her bald skin is covered with pimples. The wing pinions are left, but some of the tail quills have been lost. She holds badly in the air and instead of coming down on a small bush, she misses the branch and lands in the grass a step away from Muru. The birds must have flocked around Ure too when he passed here, screeching even louder, perhaps, because he was going to Bralgu. Yes, that is where Marngit wants him to go. The medicine man should have gone on that journey himself; he would be able to persuade our ancestors to come with help much easier, but being aged the old man feared he might never return.

My mouth is dry and hard; Muru must feel like that, too. If there is no water around he will soon pant out his last breath. The green grove is near now; there must be water there. The birds fly ahead of me and swing left, keeping a good way clear of the place, flapping their wings and screeching to tell me to do the same. Something sinister is hidden in those dark shadows—a bunch of flying foxes, perhaps. Would they scare the birds so much? Maybe it is nothing—the galahs are just glad to see me and are carrying on to show it. Animals can tell their skin relatives much sooner than humans do. Had any of the girls gone through *nara* before they were taken away? I doubt it; the fertility ceremony comes moons after the girls are taken to *nongaru* to be initiated as women. It is a pity I have not been through *nara* also, not the proper one.

When I am back in Galwan I will tell *momo* about the galahs

106

covered with pink feathers, looking as pretty and sacred as the day they were taken away. Yes, the old soul should still be there, strolling along the beach at Boma-Boma Cape. A line of boulders stretches from there far into the sea, half submerged and covered with oyster shells—all that is left of the bridge that was chewed by the monster. The old people like to hang around there so that when they die they will be near at hand for our spirits to ferry them to Bralgu.

Not far from the place where the rocks mark the path to Bralgu lies the *nara* ground. The slopes of Mount Wawalag fall short of the shore there, forming a plain with a large lagoon between the edge of the hills and the shore dunes. In the evening the lagoon looks dark, as though the shadow of the mountain has fallen that way. The thick groves of cycad palms ringing the lagoon and the pandanus forest behind it shield the place from the wind. In the middle of the day, the palm fronds rustle, showing their bright green bellies. As the wind passes over the trees sway. It looks as though wave after wave has rolled out of the sea and is traveling over the plain. The lagoon appears gray-green and seems to be at rest. It looks as though a large turtle, *dalwadbu*, has come out of the water, wandered onto the plain and chosen to rest among the weeds instead of on the sandy shore.

When I was there last I was told by *momo*, "You'll be *bala*, ["grown up"] soon and . . ." She paused for a while to add full meaning to the words. "When the next *nara* comes you'll have a good splash in the lagoon."

"Will I pound cycad nuts to feed a man?"

"Yes, the trees are laden."

"What if they don't hold *nara* this season?"

One of *momo's* cheeks twitched. "They have to, otherwise there'll be no turtle eggs, yams, fish, nuts . . . and no newborn children. The way they make the ceremony you can tell how

107

much life is going to spring up in the coming season." She never wore a waistcover to hide her shorn *diridiri*. By showing the scars, she hoped to shame the men for not doing enough to prevent the *balandas* from taking our girls away.

"What about the stone, *dugaruru*; shouldn't I have one to pound the nuts on?"

"They'll give it to you when they make you into *bala*. The initiation ceremony comes first; it'll be soon."

My face went red. "What will it be like?"

"They break your *dagu* ["vagina"], with the tip of a boomerang, then make you into a woman. You'll remember the day for the rest of your life."

"Does the man hurt you?"

Momo kept silent for a while, her face turned toward the horizon. Some distance away, beyond the foaming line of the tide and off the line of rocks, lay Durana Island, still looking like the monster but asleep and partly submerged. "Why would the man hurt you?"

"They say it bleeds when they strike you with that boomerang."

"They have to open you up."

I asked who would do that. Bungul, the man to whom I was betrothed, or perhaps someone else, a man from *jiridja*, your own relatives, but she said nothing. Girls are never told who will be the man who brings them into womanhood; they have to wait and learn it on initiation day.

Muru, we are here at last, shielded from the sun. It feels much cooler in the shade. The trees are covered with dark green leaves, so tender and damp you can squeeze water from them if there is no spring. The foliage has a shiny coat and a spongy back. I have never seen them before. Whoever planted the trees, our spirits or the *balandas*, they chose the right spot, a water hole is only a shade away. It looks grayish black—that will not matter. Several leaves, still fresh and green, have fallen off and are floating in the pool. Why does the dog shy away from the water? It . . . I'd better not try it . . . two water skinks are lying stiffly on the surface with their bellies turned up. A tortoise has tried to crawl out but only reached the bank before it ran out of strength.

A large tree, long dead, has left behind a wide space and a dry stump bigger than any I have seen before. The bark has long since peeled off, and the white wood has become stone-hard. A row of heavy bolts rings the stump, streaking it with a reddish rusty color that stands out against the light color of the trunk. There are more bolts than I and all the girls from *nongaru* could count. None of them seems to have rusted off. When they forged their bolts, the whites must have made them strong enough to last much longer than the souls chained to the tree.

A mound of charcoal—all that remains of an old fire. Over it lies the billycan. Only the handle and part of the rim are left; the rest has been eaten by rust. Tough though steel might be, it does not last forever. I should tell *momo*, poor soul. Look, several twigs have been nipped off the trees and lie scattered on the ground. Machines are no good at sneaking in and out of a place without leaving any marks. A small shady patch on the bare ground has an oily smell. The helicopter must have coughed when it was taking off and spat out a lump of dirt from its guts. This time it has done no good, either to the machine or man, coming so far into the bush.

The river seems to be a good way off, but the sun has begun to climb down. Let us go, Muru, we have another stretch of dry country to walk before quenching our thirst. Keep on, my furry friend; no dingo has ever died of thirst, and neither has a black man.

The galahs have taken to the air again; they are much quieter

109

now and only call occasionally to tell me which way to go. Yes, they want me to skirt around those barren hills of mining dirt. Not even a spirit could make his way among the pits and traps over there. The birds must have warned Ure, too, to keep away from Gin Downs and that nasty pool. A man need only take a sip from a poisoned water hole, and he will not live to tell how he felt. The whites must have found out that Ure is on his way to our spirit world; they would poison a whole sea to stop him from bringing help.

The galahs swoop twice over a pile of stones gathered on the ground before heading toward the river. There should be the same number of stones on that pile as there are bolts on that old tree. Did the whites know the stones are *dugaruru*? When she is born, each woman has *dugaruru* but begins to think of it only at the time of her first menstruation, worrying that if the stone does not come out of her *walg*, no man will ever make love to her. It is a pity I left Galwan without seeing *nara*. Had I been taken to the ceremony, I would know more about the sacred stone. The nut the women pound on it is made into *ngadu* damper, and when our men eat it they have the strength to chant, dance and make love.

When traveling from Galwan to the town, we passed farther north, through the hill country, as there was no need to follow the river line then. Ranger had a small machine that he called "go-pass" or something. It was not much to see, was hardly bigger than a watch and looked like one, but it told you which way to go. I am not sure how a small machine with no sound did that, but it must work somehow, otherwise Ranger could never have crossed all those tribal countries and found his way back home.

Ranger had his hut on Red Cliff, the same one that his father lived in when he was there, but instead of a cross, he erected a huge pole. It was quite a tree. All the Galwan men were called

110

in to drag it in from the bush and sink the trunk into the ground. A tall rod with a wire attached to it was tied on top of the pole. It was for the *balanda* to talk through. "If you put your ear against the pole you can hear a voice," I was told. The white man's boss from a faraway country often called Ranger; and no one knew enough of their lingo to say what it was all about. Yes, one of our fellows, Madaman, *momo's* husband brother, learned to talk the *balandas'* way a bit, and he often pressed one of his ears against the pole and told the others who would be the next man to get a steel ax and how much tobacco was on the way in. Madaman hung on to Doctor Cross and was often seen with a large cross on his back, walking around the hut with the *balanda* following behind, reading from an open book.

It would have been far better for *momo* if Madaman had kept away from the whites. When a man dies, his widow goes to his brother and becomes his woman; it could have been good for poor *momo*. Madaman already had three much younger women to look after, but Doctor Cross did not like it. They say the *balanda* told Madaman he already had two wives too many and that if there was one more it would make Jesus or Justice very angry. He would not send any axes or packets of tobacco ever again.

No one knew for sure what Ranger was doing in our country, though some say he was sent by his boss to look after the trees and the rocks and the Galwan people as well; that is what *momo* thought, too. Once, on our way from Nara Lagoon, we saw three men doing something near a small cliff at the mountain's lowest scarp. It was Ranger, my father and Madaman. We hid in the bushes and waited for them to go; *momo* would not have liked to meet her son running about the bush with a *balanda*. The men ran quickly along the edge of the rocks and dashed behind a boulder. A moment later the whole cliff jumped up, burst into thunder and half of it slid down into the bush below.

111

A swarm of smaller stones flew over us, stripping off pieces of bark and tearing at the leaves; a branch snapped off and fell right in front of us, lashing my face with twigs.

Soon after the dust had settled around the cliff, Ranger walked back. He had a small hammer in his hand, and he chipped a few pieces off the freshly split rock, looked at them for a while and then threw the lot inside his bag.

Momo whispered, "What did that dreadful man do to you, Wawalga?"

On the way back to our hut she said no more. We walked silently all the way to the camp, feeling as though *dal*, a powerful curse, had been placed not only on the mountain but on the people as well.

Yes, Muru, let us drink. We could splash in the water too if the day had not cooled down. I doubt if the whites would have poisoned the whole river.

I'd better stop and make camp here. There are a few big rocks where I can shelter from the night breeze. My *dudji* ("fire-sticks") are gone, both of them. They must have fallen from my bag. I'll have to make a new pair—two sticks of the right kind of dry wood—and if there is nothing better nearby, a sharp-edged stone held in the hand will scrape off all the knots and smooth the stick so that it will not make blisters on the skin. When the wood is good, fire is not far away. One stick lies on the ground and the other one has to be pressed against it and at the same time spun between the thumbs. If all goes well, smoke will pour from the wood without a single blister showing on your palms.

They call the stick that lies on the ground *dagu*, and the other that drills into it *garga*. Bringing the pair of sticks together and rubbing one into the other is the beginning of a man and a woman, so the Galwan people say. I do not know why, but the men often like to joke about it, and they tease the girls. *Momo* told me that when a woman is married she should ask only her husband to make the fire sticks, no one else. Men are a tricky lot, and you could end up without a fire but with something you did not ask for.

CHAPTER FOUR

The dog howls. Muru walks several spears behind, halting now and then to lift his snout up and call into the distance. There cannot be a soul around in the bush. Dogs can tell that much better than humans and bark or growl, but when they howl they are saying far more. They can sense bush fires, flood, plague— and how they wail when an eclipse grips the moon.

The journey has worn out the animal. He staggers over uneven ground, and at every stop he holds up one leg or another; the paws must feel sore. Come here . . . come here, poor soul. I'll give you a cuddle! He must be fed up with the long trip and has grown weary. I should have stopped at the last camp. A day or two of rest would have done some good for both of us. Galwan country will not run away however long it takes us to reach the peninsula. It was a nice stop this morning; the river forks there with many shady pools to fish in. I saw a pair of tortoises skipping into the water. No, I should not go back, there will be more good spots like that to come.

Muru claws me. There must be something he wants to tell me. You poor soul, no hair left and your skin all tender and red.

Can dogs see spirits? *Momo* thinks they can. She has been told by Marngit that dogs are our dead relatives, who were in the spirit world and have been reborn with four legs, hoping that life in this new shape might be less troublesome.

I had better move on while the shadows are still long. When the day heats up, I may have to stop for the faltering dog more often. Look, his red skin is like raw meat, but he would not be complaining about that. Dogs seldom howl for their own troubles but often worry about what might happen to humans. Once in Narku country they howled for a day and a night, a whole pack of them. "Watch out for shooting stars, one will come down," *momo* told me. We were at Mangrove Bay, her maiden *babaru* (family). I thought she was talking about the sky, not about humans, and wondered if it would have been safer if we had been in Galwan instead of Narku country.

I should wait for a while, not sitting but leaning against the tree trunk, until Muru catches his breath. He lifts his snout again, but some sudden urge stops his howling and he dashes into the bushes. The dog's skin has grown cracked and crusty, and a cluster of flies hangs around his shoulders. There, they have been brushed off now, but not for long. Once the *wurulu* smell blood it is hard to chase them off. The dogs at Mangrove Bay looked much bigger, perhaps because they had fur. Grambua, a young woman there, calls each of them by name and never throws a stone or shouts at an animal. *Momo* too thought that dogs were Narku, her *dua* people, who, after being buried long ago in those *ingabungas* have come out to join the tribe again. They are forbidden to talk so as not to pass on to us the secrets of the spirit world but they can howl, telling of trouble that is to strike.

A shadow passes over the ground; there is no cloud around to cast it, though. The leaves on the bushes flutter for a while. Dogs can see the spirits, I was told at Mangrove Bay.

115

Whatever disaster the dogs were predicting *momo* liked to stay in her *dua* country where her nephew Warinji, Grambua's husband, had a hut on the fringes of the bay, just where the western slopes of the Wawalag meet a large swamp. The mangrove forest there was crowded with birds, the nest full of eggs.

More than anything we liked *njuga* ("mud crab"). They were always there, hiding among the tangled roots, and would crawl out only if you knew how to trick them. I often went with Benima, Grambua's sister, a girl of my own age, to the swamp and struggled through knee-deep mud, but it did not take you long to turn up a good catch if you knew how. Grambua cooked them in water; *momo* liked them that way. You leave stones on the fire until they get red hot, and then you chuck them into a paperbark bucket or a hollow stump filled with water and crabs. The water steams and boils for a while, and when it all cools down *njuga* are ready to be eaten.

Muru, keep your eyes open for *djanda* ("goanna"); there should be some in the bush around here, and just one will do us. Held over the fire for a while, a goanna's fat melts quickly, and when it cools I will rub you with it. It heals everything; you'll feel reborn, my furry friend.

The dog points his snout toward the bush. That shadow is back, though it hardly moves now. It has the shape of a bearded man holding a spear and a boomerang.

I had better walk away from the river, the reptiles are more likely to be in the sun than in the shade. For all its abundance of food, Mangrove Bay has few goannas. They might keep away from the swampy plain where it floods during the monsoon. Humans do not like wet either; they raise their huts higher above the ground in Narku country than anywhere else. Warinji built his hut on stilts, too. Fully grown trees were used as *darbal* ("fork posts"), with a number of saplings laid across between them and tied with bark ropes to form a platform.

There was a roof above made of sheets of bark and leafy branches. They needed one, for Grambua was to have a child. Her belly was not showing yet, but it would be soon, and they were hurrying in case the child chose to come during the Wet.

The sun is hard on Muru. I have to break off a branch and keep the flies off his back. Hold on, furry friend, it'll not be long now; that stuff cures everything. Marngit carries goanna fat in his bag; I saw a coconut shell full of it when he came down to help Grambua. Hold on, Muru, I have to brush those pests of flies off you. That woman was worse off than you. She was found on the beach after being unconscious for a day and a night. When she woke up she could not say much or stand up. Wariŋji and Magani carried her on a mat all the way from Warngi Inlet to the hut. She smelled like the empty bottles you find around the shore where the barge always anchors when it calls in with the supplies.

She had eaten the wrong food, *momo* thought. When a woman is expecting a child there are many kinds of tucker she has to keep away from: a joey from the wallaby's pouch is not to be eaten, nor a young chick, and many other foods. Marngit thought that, too. He had a strange-looking spear-thrower in the shape of a long pipe, made from a hollow log and fringed at one end with a circle of human hair. He carried his bag; I could not see what was in it, but he took out a half coconut shell full of goanna fat, pressed it against Grambua's body and chanted for a while. His voice was low at first, then he stood up, held the shell in both hands and, pointing it at Mount Wawalag, called out loudly. "She has eaten *balanda* food. Oh, forgive her, she'll be a good mother." The voice sounded so clear that I could almost see each of the words floating through the air above the paper-bark trees, passing the gum forest and the hilly slope behind it, reaching the mountain peak and then moving beyond it, right across the sea of Bralgu, where the spirits go but where man has

117

sometimes been taken.

At my age I should not have been allowed to hear Marngit's magic chants, not before becoming *bala*; even *momo*, his sister, had to move a few shades away from the camp. But as she could not see, no one made her go any farther. As for me, I was regarded as being nothing more than her *mauwulan* ("walking stick"). I held my hands over my eyes, but. . . I could not help parting my fingers a little to peep at the scene, expecting Grambua to rise to her feet at any moment. Marngit called "Bugalili!" several times, chanted for a while and rubbed goanna fat hard into her skin, but nothing startling happened. The spirits are not to be rushed into doing favors. Even when it means a life, they always need time to think it over; that is what *momo* believed.

The dog stares at the shadow, which drifts slowly alongside our track. A dilly bag is visible now, too, dangling from the man's neck. Would Marngit recognize me now that I have grown into a woman? He ought to know every one of us and be able to tell which *babaru* ("family") each tribal soul comes from, for he has to direct the spirits when they bring *djuwei* ("unborn children") into the woman's womb. "Without us to bear, there'll not be any tribes," *momo* said.

I should keep closer to the river now, where the shade from the gums is thicker and the sandy ground is not so hard to walk on. Some of the trees here have grown tall, with the top branches tucked under the blue mat of the sky. There must have been a tribe of people living here once. They say that when a tree grows high, there is a man's spirit in it that hurries toward the sky to see the country around. It is good that there are trees here; I can walk during the hottest part of the day as far as the shade lasts. Let us hope that I am on the right track. It would be sad if, after following the river for so many camps and making such a tiring journey, I reached a country that is not mine, after all.

118

Muru must be feeling much better now; he looks at me and wags his tail. It will be good if the animal does not lick that goanna fat off or roll in the dust for a while. Now that the red skin is soft, it will heal faster. I should use that stuff on myself, too, the skin of my feet is rock hard, and when I walk over stones I make a sound like a *balanda* in boots. The goanna fat helped Grambua. The child that was going to be born never came, but long after the Wet she began to move about with the help of *mauwulan* ("walking stick") and had to keep out of the mangroves where she could be stuck forever in the mud. Whatever did the harm, the white man's grog or the food she had eaten, Marngit and his chanting helped. "He only fails when the spirits are angry," I was told.

The dog is dragging behind again, holding his head up but whining instead of howling. The animal senses something for sure. There might be a ceremonial ground or sacred water hole; I must be careful where I walk. I have not seen any humans, but there are spirits around and places like this are dearer to them than to anyone else. People are not happy seeing a strange woman strolling about. Men are secretive, and they like to think that they are the only ones who know what the world should look like and have their say when the youngsters are grown up enough to become *bala*.

Look, the river has weakened suddenly. Only scattered pools of water remain on the bed of bare pebbles and rocks. The water might . . . no, I doubt if it seeps through the ground; the trees that cling to the banks do not seem to grow so well and look much paler than those I saw before. Beyond them stretches open country, with stunted bushes and fewer leaves clinging to almost stripped branches. The patches of barren land have widened. It will not be long now. A camp or two upstream and the river will change into a dry creek bed. Let us hope it leads me right. Am I on the right track?

119

The dog stops and whines again. Muru feels the dry, hilly country ahead and is trying to warn me of the hard time to come. It is a pity I cannot stay and camp for several days down at that river junction. There is no need to rush. Galwan, my *jiridja* country, will be there whenever I come back and . . . yes, I will have to go to Narku to look for Bungul. He was already aging when I was there, but that is why I am to be his woman. Someone has to look after him . . . and his women, too.

A gust hits a grove suddenly, tossing leaves and bushes in the air. The dust has risen, too. It is hard to see that shadow again, though it should not be far off; the spirits can come and go at will. Let's keep going, my furry friend.

When I get there a camp may already be set up; the spirits often let your relatives and friends know what has happened. I will have to rest for a few days and then start looking for food. They will all be getting old now. I am glad *momo* often took me to Mangrove Bay. Now I know how to catch crabs and where to look for yams; there is plenty of food in the mangrove swamps and paperbark bush. The creeks run down from the hills, and before they reach the bay they branch out into many small pools. During high tide the fish wander into these small inlets and then, as the sea draws back, stay trapped in the shallow, muddy water. They gather in the swampy claypans left behind, and it is not hard to catch them. Bungul's two wives, Yinguamba and . . . I forget the name of the other one . . . what food would they like best?

The dog walks away from the riverbank. There must be something out in the scrub, for he wags his tail as though he sees a Galwan soul. No voice or sound is to be heard. The dry country is silent for a while, then a willy-willy springs up. The dust and leaves whirl about for a while in the air, mounting into a column sky high. The column is shaped in the form of an

120

bearded old man holding a spear and a boomerang. Yes, he has a spear-thrower made from a hollow log. That dilly bag still dangles from his neck as he drifts across the land. Muru whines and wags his tail, then walks slowly after the willy-willy. I had better follow him.

Yes, I must have been on the wrong track ever since that river junction. Good, Marngit is going to lead us across the country to the other fork of the river. It should not take long to get on the right track again. Spirits know the way much better than humans.

CHAPTER
FIVE

I should press on toward the horizon if this journey is ever to take me to Galwan. The hot day does not help much, especially when you are moving over hills of bare rocks baking in the sun. A long, narrow passage snakes across the country, dodging the bluffs. It is good there is a track to follow, for without it a man would be like a mere grain of sand.

We'll make it, Muru, my furry friend. Look at that mushroom-shaped cliff over there; its top sticks out like the brim of a large hat resting on a narrow neck of rock, battered by wind and sun. Let's hope a willy-willy does not suddenly tear along the gorge; if it comes down, that cliff will cut off the passage.

I may have been here before, you know. Not with Ranger, on my own. The trip from Galwan to town seemed shorter then, perhaps because I was younger or . . . fear stops you from bothering about how long a journey takes. Yes, it does. In country like this, as dry as red-hot rock, one travels like a crab. It is not that the body wears away, but the mind grows blank. It becomes like *gara* ("stone blade"), and you cannot decide whether it is safer to press on with the journey or to move about only at dawn and sunset when the air is much kinder. Look, a man is up there, standing on that mushroom bluff, almost on the edge of the rim. From the sky behind him a bright cloud bounces back the sun's blaze. No face could be seen against that light.

Keep on, Muru, there should be a water hole beside that mushroom-shaped rock. We must stop there for a while to cool off after a good drink. It will be a long stretch—a camp or two, perhaps—before the track takes us to the next one. I have camped here, yes! It was thundering then, the whole sky shattered by lightning; that hardly ever happens during the Dry. Maybe the storm was trying to catch Ranger. I felt that Marngit might have chanted the right words to Djanbuwal to come and punish the white man and scare me. Look, Muru. I camped under that outcrop of rock. The charcoal from the fire is still there, but the wind has blown away most of the ashes. That stone over there . . . I used it for pounding the roots of bushes I gathered from the sandy ground. Two bulbs lie on the ground, withered and shrunken. They could have been pulled up only days ago; anything left on the hot sand dries out fast. Men would rather hunt than gather roots, but when you are hurrying back to your world to muster some help, you will grab any food the country can spare. I must be following Ure's track.

The dog is gasping for a drink. He has dashed into the water hole and is scratching the dry rocks. There is no moisture to attract him, but the animal might have been lured by the water mark left behind from the last rain, moons ago. Come out, furry. There should be something else around here to quench our thirst. No black soul has ever died from lack of water, not in our country.

The old man is still up there. He holds a lump of red clay, *maidja,* and a pair of newly made armbands; the cockatoo feathers look brighter than the cloud in the background. I can

123

see myself there too, resting on that cloud just as a girl would stretch out on the sand for her body to be smeared for the ceremony. The man looks down to the gorge, nodding to me to go around to the shady side of the bluff. Come on, Muru. Look for deep shade behind the boulders where we can rest. Later we will look for bulbs to quench our thirst with, just as Ure did when he passed through here. There will still be some left in the ground along the gorge. Ure hardly left any trace; he must have dragged a branch behind him to sweep the ground. When they are tracking any of us, the *balandas* often sniff around the water hole, though on a long run a man quickly learns how to go around them. No, Ure is not such a fool as to walk into it.

The rock shelter stretches along the wall of the gorge, and as it swings around, a bluff leads the way out of the sun into the cool shade. I did not go that way last time. It might rain. Yes, my furry friend, the rain could come again. You should have seen it when I was here last time. The gorge turned into a river. I did not need the water hole to drink from; the sky bucketed a whole torrent over me.

Large drawings cover the wall of the rock shelter, some of them blurred by the bright light, others veiled by shadows. Most of them show a large *urban* ("emu"), often without any legs because the part of the boulder under it has eroded down into the gorge. The bird must be *marain* ("totem of a tribe who lived here"). Down in the shady shelter more pictures line the wall. They look old: the color has almost faded away, leaving only a blurred outline. I had better not touch them; they will be sacred, too.

From the shady side of the bluff appears a small flat gully tucked among the hills. In the middle lies a pile of dug earth; the white soil blazes in the sun. Above it is a boiling haze of melting air.

There I am, lying on the sand or on the melting air; the heat is

124

*the same. The old man hands me the armbands. Never have the
cockatoo feathers looked so white as on the day of initiation. The
elder helps me put on my* maidja—*the same one I wore at* nongaru; momo *made it for me. The strings, left a bit hard, pinch the
skin on my breast. That hardly matters; the old man has mixed
the red clay with kangaroo fat already, and takes some of it from
a coconut shell to rub my skin. "I should have mixed some* gulan
*with it." He sounds as if he is one of our elders. My thighs have
been smeared. The old hand rubs my belly now, leaving a rim of
thick ocher around my navel. The hand moves farther; my breasts
do not look fully grown yet—the two bulbs seen at the foot of the
bluff, though smeared now. "Life will come again—let's soak
you well."*

The old man, with the help of his spear, walks slowly across
the gully toward the bluff. Near the pile of dug earth the
balandas had also left behind an oily patch on the ground and
two empty metal drums. It is hard to tell from the heat haze if he
walks over or around them.

The dog is about to whine but changes its mind suddenly and
wags its tail instead. The old man heads slowly toward the
shelter, his bare feet making hardly any noise on the hard
ground; but his spear shaft, used as a walking stick, clatters
against the rocks. His eyes look clouded. It is good that Muru is
quiet; no tribal soul wants to be barked away when they are here
to help. I should say something. The shelter looks more sacred
than I am able to tell. "Forgive me for walking in *marain*
place."

The old man leans his spear against the wall and sits down in
the shade with his back against the rocks. The long beard looks
strikingly white now. Yes, it has grown in the shape of a sea
shell; it hardly moves when the words come out of the mouth.
"You had to come."

Below the white beard hangs a small dilly bag; the weight

125

makes it rest firmly on his chest, partly covering the initiation marks on the dark skin. Those marks can tell you the lingo, tribe and *babaru*. It is like looking into the face of a man.

"Are there many of our people around here?"

The clouded eyes have suddenly grown wet. "Tribes of them are scattered along the Milky Way track."

He would know when Ure had passed through. "What happened to our people?"

An old, withered hand reached for the dilly bag, took out a few pebbles and held them on his palm. "Many of them are here, shrunk now, ground by the wind and the sand."

"That water hole—has it been dry for long?"

"It has to stay like that; the *balandas* are often around to chuck poison into it."

A headbelt holds his gray hair back; it looks like the one of *nongaru* ground, woven in many colors like a rainbow. Perhaps it is the same sacred garment. Marngit would only wear it when the girls were brought to the initiation billabong to be "opened" with the tips of boomerangs. He will wear it again later during *nara*, when both the tribes gather around Dalwadbu Lagoon to plead with the spirits to make everything fertile; not just the girls but turtles, plants and everything else in the bush that can bring new life.

"How many of us have passed through here?"

"No woman has gone back lately. I hoped you would come; rest for a while, my *wirgul*. There is fresh sand in the shelter." Marngit rose slowly, took two oval stones from his bag and, clapping them to accompany his call, chanted into the distance: "Bugalili! Bugalili! . . . ," just as he did on *nongaru* ground in Galwan so long ago.

Something unseen floats in the air, the walls of the shelter brighten. A tall man painted with tribal patterns holds a spear high above his head, hooked on the thrower's peg and ready to launch, while at the same time he swings around with *galdj*

126

("stone ax"). Above his elbows two *galamba* look like ours made of possum fur and cockatoo feathers with long tassels of wild cotton; whenever they appear in ceremonial paintings the armbands are shown like a pair of shooting stars. Small honeycomb patterns of white, red and yellow cover the ancestor's chest, telling of the many tribes and different lingos that came from him.

"Bugalili, bugalili . . ." The call echoes from somewhere.

That man painted on the wall is Wudal surely, our ancestor from the Dreaming. His legs are shaped like a boomerang, floating in the air while his *garga* ("penis") hangs down from between his thighs, thick and long as a python; it touches the ground. The penis has sprung out to the opposite slab, and the figure of a woman sits on it. Inside her *dagu* is the head of a python sucking blood from the womb. The woman could be Garangal, one of the two Wawalag sisters that Wudal made love to. The elders say that when the sisters were on their journey, they saw Wudal stretched out on his back, asleep under a tree. They giggled while they decided which one of the two should approach him. The man slept with his *garga* erect like a python; Garangal crept near and sat on it. Then, with the lovemaking over, she left quietly without waking him. What a pity I did not ask *momo* to tell me more about the story; perhaps I could have learned if the Wawalag gave birth before or after she met Wudal. Look, I must have walked into *nongaru*, the "ceremonial place" of the tribe that lived here.

In Galwan, the girls are initiated, not in a cave but at *nongaru*, the ground near the billabong at the top end of Gunga River. Our men tell the story of the first lovemaking rather differently by painting Wudal on a sheet of bark. They, too, often like to show man's *garga* in the shape of a python, but it is the best they can do; woman is the the only one who can bear children.

"Bugalili! Bugalili! Bugalili! . . ." The chant is always there

127

to call for the start of the ceremony.

The red color should mean clouds scattered about the sky like boulders lit by the rage of a bush fire. Like an opening in the land, the sky widens and slopes slowly away toward the place where the sun has plunged into the sea to camp. That is how the men in Galwan know that the first showers are about and they can tell that the flickering tongue of the lightning snake and the rolling thunder behind will bring on the Wet.

The men like to think that they are the ones who make the clouds spring up on the horizon. They go to a lot of trouble to make boomerangs for the occasion and stain them with the red color they have dug out of the ground. The boomerangs, a whole row of them, are lined up to face the north wind. When it comes, they say it will wake up Julungul, the mighty python who sleeps in the sacred water hole, and tell him that the young girls from the country are on the way to *nongaru* to be pierced by boomerangs. As soon as the virgin blood is spilt, Julungul will hurry along the clouds for the monsoon rain to wash the red stain from the grass and fronds and drain the lure into the billabong. It happens every year at the end of the Dry season, to bring new life not only to humans but to the country as well.

I still hear a chant floating through the Galwan country. It is like the sweet smell of nectar that is to come.

They are always there, men chipping at wooden boomerangs:
Men of the southern clans, of the barramundi and catfish . . .
Chips of wood fly out, from shaping the wooden boomerangs . . .
They are always there, women moving their buttocks . . .
Men chipping and shaping boomerangs, flattening their sides . . .
They think of the *nongaru* place, of the sacred ground . . .
They are always there, men of the southern tribes:
Clans from the Julungul country, men with subincised penises . . .

The men might be wrong. *Momo* thinks that it is not their boomerangs and chanting that bring the rain but Wanba, the

128

Morning Star Pigeon, who does it all by sounding out his call. He lets the ancestors know that the clouds are needed to bring the thirsty country back to life again. The bird lives on *nongaru*, and when it coos at the right time of year, the mellow sound floats like a spear through the air and reaches Bralgu. That is how our ancestors there are told that the last blade of grass has dried out, the leaves have dropped from the trees and the country, worn out like a hunted beast, is fighting for its last breath. Djanbuwal is always the one to master the clouds far beyond the horizon, but he will send no rain until Galwan men gather on the ceremonial ground to ask for it in the proper way.

They make the boomerangs, chipping the defloration point . . .
Thinking about the dancing and rites of the *kunapipi*.
Men of the southern clans, and the Cockatoo tongue . . .
Thinking about the *mandiela*, the sacred dancing,
For now the boomerangs are nearing completion:
Spirits and people, men from the southern clans . . .
Thinking while they chip away at the boomerangs . . .
Flattening the sides, making the point for deflowering girls . . .
Clans from the Julungul country, all assembled together . . .
In that sacred place, in the middle of the *nongaru*.

The stones on the ground in the shelter have been swept; the sand Marngit brought in looks clean—no pebbles or small twigs to hurt your skin. There are no caves at our *nongaru*, the Galwan and Narku men have built *murlg* ("hut") instead, large enough to shelter the girls of all the coastal and inland tribes. There is no fine sand to be found near the billabong; the men have to bring it from the seashore for each ceremony. You can see the small shells and the specks of crystal on the soft ground as you lie under the bark roof of *murlg*. The shells look much like those at Warngi Inlet, too far perhaps to be carried to *nongaru*. However, *momo* says they would bring it from beyond the sunset to make sure that when the women lie in the shade there

129

will be nothing to harm them.

Leaving his spear behind, Marngit has walked down into the cave. I cannot see him, but his voice is still clear: "Bugalili! Bugalili! Bugalili!" Yes, this must be it; you can wander all your life through the country—from one sunset to another—but there is only one place and the right day for *djuwei*, that speck of life, to be brought to you to mother.

There I am again lying on the melting air over the sand; my thighs are widely stretched. The breeze meddles with the tangled mound of my diridiri, *the wind whirls, tickling* maularin, *the lips below. "Bugalili! Bugalili—come to life again!" The boomerang claps against a spear shaft.*

The python has moved away from the painting in the rock shelter and undulates over the hot sand. His head rears while the long tongue flickers to taste the wind, the scent of saliva coming from the open dagu.

Above the white sand everything melts; my body turns into a pool of saliva, reddish though. Everything coming from walg *looks red. That is why they smear the skin and boomerang with that color.*

The flickering tongue of the python licks my maularin, *the skin around* dagu *looks terribly red—that too might melt soon. The clapping of the boomerang hastens; that bearded old man seems to be in a hurry. All spirits are a bit restless with the life-making rituals. The python feels immense; the skin of* dagu *stretches to the limit to let him through. Though the air around still melts, the serpent's head is seen clearly. It ejects something. Yes, out has come* djuwei, *hardly bigger than a fly. The* walg *hollows to make room for new life.*

I feel . . . my *walg* has become warm and . . . swollen slightly. If I keep my eyes closed I can see inside it. Yes, it is like peeping inside a kangaroo pouch. *Djuwei*, that tiny spirit, has suddenly grown into *wadu*, a little child no bigger than a

130

cocoon, still and silent. They say that only a mother and the spirits can tell it is there. Tiny as it might look, with us to mother the young life, and the spirit world to care for it, the child will grow into a hunter. Without that, and that alone, there would be no black man, and perhaps not even trees would grow in the country.

CHAPTER SIX

The rocks cool down fast from the day-long struggle with the sun, and soon the reptiles will crawl back into their holes. If a man stays still as the dark falls he can hear the unfolding of the withered leaves. Marngit would have no time for listening to the bush; he moves some paces ahead of me, his bearded head and the shaft of his spear silhouetted against a light patch of sky above the craggy line of the bluffs. Spirit or human, the medicine men know the country as well as their skin. Where is he taking me? "We will follow the Milky Way track," I was told a while ago, and I have heard no word since.

I could have stayed at the cave; there might have been a water hole in the hills where I could have hung around for several days. Galwan country is still many camps away, but once you have seen our ancestors painted on the rocks, then black man's country has been reached, even if not your tribal people. Farther up the track should be Muruwul water hole, where the sisters gave birth to the first tribal man. Yes, Marngit must be in a hurry to show me the place; it is like taking you back to see your own *walg*.

132

When we stop to rest I should tell him about the center and all that happened in the enclosure. Perhaps he knows about it already. I doubt if Marngit would like to hear about Doctor Cross and Ranger; mentioning *balandas'* names makes every tribal elder angry. "They're like brooding *baru* ("crocodiles") gathering their clutch," *momo* told me. When our men rushed to Red Cliff to storm the corrugated iron shade the white man lived in, I watched Gunbuna, Bungul and the others swinging their *barlait* ("clubs") against the wireless mast, shouting all the swear words you can think of. Someone cut off the wire, and Madaman yelled into it; the others joined in but no *balanda* voice answered back. Gunbuna, not so old and slow then, struck the pole with an ax and the others rushed in, each eager to give a blow. Then they carried the pole up the cliff and tossed it down into the sea. The men were angry because one of our girls was being taken away in the barge. They felt broody all right. It was only the day before we were all due for *nongaru* to be initiated. You do not let any of your clutch get lost then!

I should hurry on; the medicine man has moved a way off now. I can still hear his footsteps, though, and a clicking noise. Yes, it is the spear shaft knocking against the rocks as he uses it as a walking stick. Far ahead of him a light blinks in the dark. Too low to be a star, it shows only now and then, appearing from behind bushes or boulders as you walk over the uneven ground. A campfire? It will be one of us; the spirits know whoever journeys along the track, and without their help a soul would never make it through.

Ure was there too when they stormed the *balanda's* hut, for the girl was Benima, his cousin. The men would have flattened that hut and thrown the last piece of corrugated iron into the sea if it had not been for *baba*, my father. Ranger sent him to tell the tribal elders that he had just had word from his big boss that Benima would be brought back if our fellows calmed down.

133

The seaman from the barge was to be handed over to us too, tied in chains. The whites certainly know how to slip out of a mess easily, like a fish from a slimy hand.

Marngit waits for a while to listen to the night, then the walking stick begins to clatter against the rocky ground again as he heads toward the distant light. During that raid on Ranger's place Ure must have had a spear instead of *barlait* ("club"); he never parts with it. Even while he is sleeping one of his hands always climbs to the shaft. His father, Gunbuna, thinks that Djanbuwal often comes at night to tell Ure how to make the best of that weapon; one day he might be able to handle *larban* like our mighty ancestor does. I saw Ure on *nongaru* leading a group of young men while they danced. What a sight that was! The fellows held their spears with one hand on the end of the shaft while the other grasped *gara* ("stone blade"), and while they danced the spear arched over their heads like a rainbow. They call it *malngud*, "two arms," way; it might not do much good in fighting, but it shows man as master of his tools, and while the feet stamp down, raising a cloud of dust, the spear bounces over the head. Yes, it looks like a cloud hovering over the trees, and it makes the rain come.

On both arms, just above the elbows, I had *galamba*, the "bands made of possum fur," and I was wearing my *maidja* ("string breast girdle") for the first time. *Momo* helped me make it from softened pandanus leaves. If the breast are not supported by a belt when we are dancing they will bounce. We are all called *marain* ("sacred and pretty") until the time comes to step onto the ceremonial ground. Then one has to look and behave like a woman ready to take a man from *nongaru* who, by custom, will make love to her and as many women as they can while their strength lasts. It was like that not only in my mother's and grandmother's time, but since the beginning of the black *mala* ("people"). The Wawalag sisters, Balari and Garangal, did

134

it too, while they traveled across the country setting up the black man's customs; then they came to Muruwul water hole and gave birth to the first tribal child.

A creek runs from the hills into a billabong fringed with clumps of tall palms laden with nuts. Young frond shoots strive for the sky. They are mirrored in the water like green spears tickling the fat belly of a cloud. The sun is down there on the water hole bottom to warm Julungul, the python. Under the water the spirits of all tribal souls are waiting to be born.

Down into the creek trickles gulan, *coloring the water.*

Nothing much has changed since the Wawalag's time, nor have any of their words on how to set up the initiation ceremony been forgotten. It all began with Wanba, the Morning Star Pigeon, calling for new life to come to the sun-baked country. For the clouds to appear, however, the tribes have to gather at *nongaru* first and spill *marain* ("maiden, blood"). Only then will the first showers come, not so much to quench the earth, sucked dry by the sun, but to wash the blood away and wake up Julungul, who is asleep in the billabong. The snake, lured by the sacrament, will summon more clouds and as the monsoon begins, Djanbuwal will arrive riding on the storm. Without the ancestors to bring the rain, the country will turn into rock, not even fit for a thistle or a scorpion.

The light has grown, a bright ball floating in an immense sea of dark. Come on, Muru, we had better hurry. I might lose sight of Marngit if we lag too far behind. He walks too fast for an old soul with cloudy eyes. Why do the old people go like that; they say it is trachoma or whatever word the *balandas* have for it. Wagudi thinks that as soon as the land is stripped of the trees and the rocks turn into sand the eyes grow milky, for if a man sees the naked country, he will not be able to live through the pain. It is a pity the white man's curse has caught up with Marngit, too. The medicine man knows all about tribal customs; he has been

135

master of more initiation ceremonies than many of our fellows can remember. At *nongaru* he led the girls out to *murlg*; shyly we moved on, with *galnamiri*—our bodies smeared with red and rubbed with kangaroo fat. The dance began. Across the ground stretched *ganala* ("dug-out trench") representing a mythological creek, and it ran into a pit meant to be Muruwul water hole, the *walg* of black man.

Behind us men, each holding a boomerang, stepped onto *nongaru*, too. The sound of *didjeridu* and clapping sticks bounced back from the edge of the forest and echoed across the still water of the billabong; so did the chanting.

They bring close the pointed boomerang, raising her thighs onto the
    hips of a man . . .
Pushing her down, that young girl smeared with red ocher, raising her
    thighs . . .
They think of the boomerang, with its flattened point . . .
Pushing her down, that girl, onto a man's hips, into the
    branches . . .
Young girl, smeared with red ocher and kangaroo fat . . .
Pushing her down into the branches, into the shade of the *nongaru*
They bring close the point of the boomerang, into her vulva . . .
Into the young girl smeared with red ocher, girls of the barramundi
    clans . . .
Girls crying out, pierced by the flattened point of the
    boomerang . . .

Around the ceremonial ground, the branches have been placed together to make *dagu* ("women's shade"), where each of us had to retire with her man for a short spell. *Momo* told me that my *gurung* ("partner"), would tell me when I should follow him. I was not to forget to squeal while he made love to me, and as soon as it was over I was to return to the ground, join the dancers again and be on the lookout for a new call. Something

136

must have gone wrong. I sensed it and felt afraid. Most of the girls have been led out to *dagu*, and when they returned to the ground again they pummelled their bellies and stamped hard with their feet to release *yudu*, the "semen" the men left inside them. No one has called me to go, however; my friend Malabin was trying to tell me something, but her whisper was drowned among the voices— "Bugalili!"—and the roar of *didjeridu*. She brought her mouth closer to my ear, but I had no time to make out the words. The call must have reached her from her *gurung* at that very moment, and she quickly followed the man away from the ground and disappeared behind *dagu*. The screen of the women's shade was badly made with only a few branches, and through some withered leaves I could see Malabin lying on her back, the man mounted on her with his legs and feet flexed, pressing down on her. She kept her arms stretched outward on the ground, but the man held his around her shoulders and . . . sheltering her face—*bangduman* ("open legs")—the men call it. My mind became hot and, still dancing, I kept drifting toward the edge of *nongaru* ground to get a better view. "Bugalili!" the voices yelled loudly. For a moment I thought they were shouting at me, and I felt as if my knees were about to give way and let me down. Then I realized the men were directing their calls toward the billabong and far beyond it to call up the spirits.

A rumbling comes from the darkness now. It is a strange roaring, muffled by distance, and although it is far away, you sense a slight tremor, though it is hard to say whether it comes from the ground or the air. Muru feels it too; he often stops and whines at the light.

Nothing seems to worry Marngit, though. Will Ure have any water for us? Yes, that should be him up there; he has made a big fire to show us the way. What a pity he threw that canvas bag away before he left town; he might have found something else to

137

carry water in, though. We need only a handful each to wet our throats, then when we lie on the ground to sleep we will dream of a whole swamp. He might have gathered some bulbs again and crushed them to squeeze a drop or two of moisture out. Not to worry, there will be something to drink; a man never dies of thirst in his own country. Led by the spirits we could not be on the wrong track.

The rumbling grows louder. Something is there, rolling over the hills in the dark. Perhaps Ure is bringing Djanbuwal with him. No lightning flashes in the sky, but surely it will come. The ancestor sounds busy making his *larbans*, "bundles" of them. Do you hear that, Muru, the pounding of rocks and the clattering of the chips? There is a hill called Nilibidi, in the Stone country around here; every hunter has heard of it. The Wawalags stopped there on their journey to collect a bagful of *ngambi* ("sacred flints"). Those stones make good *gara*. That is what our ancestor is doing right now. Ure has made a large fire so that Djanbuwal can see to chip the stones. Yes, you can easily hit your fingers when making the tools sharp. As soon as the spears are ready, the two men will set off. The whites have a lot to answer for; they have even fleeced you, furry. Those bloody mongrels! I doubt if the *balandas* will know the storm is gathering; Djanbuwal might take them by surprise, he likes to strike at night or in the late afternoon. I have seen him several times tearing across the sky over town, knocking down power poles, tossing trees from one side of the road to the other and blowing roofs off houses. That was just a warning, surely. This time, with a gut full of anger, he could be out to flatten the white man's world.

A newly made hut at the billabong looks too small for the Wawalags. The dog sits outside by a campfire. No dog likes to be out on a stormy night. In the hut one of the sisters lies on the ground and whimpers. Her thighs are messed with blood; the

138

ground is messed with it, too. The hut leaks and the rain drips into a red puddle.

Marngit has slowed down. I can still see him moving, but I cannot hear his footsteps or his stick any longer. I had better tiptoe, too. The light is shining on a steel tower with a white man working on a platform. Every now and then a sharp metallic sound cuts through the still mass of the dark, followed by heavy pounding. Not far from the tower, two men are sitting under a small awning, each sipping from a bottle. Behind them lies a pile of freshly dug earth, half sunk in the night mist. Perhaps they are drilling. The *balandas* are so keen to find out what is under the ground that they do not even stop to sleep. It often makes you think that the white men are not after rocks or whatever else is hidden in the ground but are sweating to dig a pit to hurry into it, as if the whole world was rushing to an end. They are either too busy or are enjoying themselves too much to notice us. If Muru makes a noise they might hear it, but the dog is a dingo and they seldom bark. Animals have learned, just as we have, not to stick their necks out, knowing that you have a chance only so long as you keep out of the white man's way.

Marngit reaches out for my hand and leads me to a water tank. It is right down at the bottom of the metal tower, so close you can feel the ground trembling like a dying snake. It is good to be black in the dark; if you can control your breathing and be silent, they will never know that you have ever been there. The water is slimy and it tastes oily, but it is wet and kills your thirst just the same. One of the whites comes to the edge of the platform and leans against the railing; he moves his hand across his forehead to wipe the sweat from his skin. A shooting star slides out of the sky over the dark field, leaving behind a trail of light that ends right above the white man's shoulder. Djanbuwal! This must be his last warning!

One of the men under the awning chucks an empty bottle

into the darkness; he is going to say something . . . Plonk! He has grown a beard since I last saw him. The hair is hardly long enough to cover his skin, but it makes him look darker and less freckled. He is struggling for words while his head jerks, then without having said anything, he reaches for another bottle. That canvas hat!

Muru claws me to go; the rattling of that rig must be hard on the dog's ears. The sound of the metal makes all of us afraid. I will hurry and catch up with Marngit. He must feel happier, too, the farther we are from the drilling site. The sight of the pile of dug-out rocks has driven him away fast. It is like seeing the ripped-open belly of your own mother. What are the whites up to with Plonk? He knows nothing about rocks!

The *balandas* might think that by having Plonk around they will please our spirits and keep Djanbuwal away, for he will not harm a man of his skin. Just wait—the whites might be in for a surprise. Wagudi told me that only children born in the tribal country can take part in our ceremonies and share *ranga* ("sacred objects of their family and clan"). Each of them is ensured of a place at the bottom of the billabong for the spirit to go after the body dies, and of the right to go to Bralgu and to be reborn. The tribal people have these privileges, for we have all come from *djuwei*, those tiny spirits brought back to life again. No man makes children in our world, although the whites do. Yes, that mob breeds differently, but that will not give a scrap of land to Plonk.

I cannot see Marngit, though he should not be far away; the clattering of his walking stick tells me which way to go. I never got around to asking him why they call this track the Milky Way. *Momo* talked about that often, too; she remembered most of the camps, counting them with pebbles—a whole pile of them. I never thought that I would be traveling on the track, too. Whatever its name might mean, it should soon come to

140

Muruwul water hole. Yes, Marngit would not miss a place like that. I might camp there for several days; the rest will do the dog and me good.

I wish there was some water to wet my mouth with. The dry rocks are not much help. An armful of leaves from the bushes could be crushed to give us a drop or two to hold off our thirst a while. It takes too long to crush them, though. No, I would rather hurry on and reach Muruwul before the day heats up.

It is a pity I had to stop last night. I hoped we might reach the water hole; the long walk is wearing us both out. That was a short rest but a good one. I sat on the ground with my back against a warm boulder, and I was dreaming before there was time to stretch out on the sand. I rested one hand on my belly while I talked to *wadu*, the "child," about Muruwul water hole. I have often seen the place when I was in Galwan, painted on a sheet of bark; it looked green and shady. A creek runs from Nilibidi Hill into the water hole, with a cluster of *marin* ("cabbage palms") sheltering the sacred pool. The elders often arrange colors on a sheet of bark to show *gulan* ("blood spilt from *dagu*"), though they seldom like to talk about the birth. "Most of it is *marain*," they often claim. It might not be so: in the old time women were the bosses of our world, but the fellows prefer to keep quiet about that now. The Wawalag sisters made spears, built huts, organized the first ceremonies and later, much later, they journeyed to Bralgu to ask Djanbuwal to come to *nara* and bring the monsoon rain with him. From Bralgu, the sisters brought back *badi* ("dilly bag") with magic power to bring plants and animals to life—the same one Marngit carries now.

Being brought up in Narku, *momo* was told different things about the Wawalags; *dua* people held that it was the sisters' brother, Djanbuwal, who made love to them, not Wudal, who I

141

saw painted in that cave. In the old time it was not *ngurubilga* ("wrong") to sleep with someone from your own *babaru*. There were no other black men in the country then, anyhow.

Once, while the sisters were making their ceremony and chanting for men, plants and animals to come to life, the brother crept in behind them and snatched their *badi* full of *ranga*, "the sacred objects that help to make life." From then onward, men made the sacred ceremonies and kept women out of it. Men cannot bear children—that is something they did not snatch from the bag. When the times comes for a spirit to be reborn and it wants to come to life as a human, not a tree or an animal, then it chooses a woman. If there are none of us around, the men can play with their *garga* and spread *yudu* ("semen") around, but not even a fly will grow from that muck.

I have not seen Marngit since morning; something must have made him hurry on to Galwan or Bralgu. He has left his footprints on the sandy ground for me to follow. It will be a while before anyone else passes here again, and time and the wind will wear away our tracks as they have so many before. Our people will always travel along the track, as they have ever since the Wawalags passed through here. Look, there is a cluster of palms. A few trunks are bare already; they are standing alone, like a pole stuck in the dry ground. They remind me of a group of wailing widows I saw somewhere, dreamed perhaps.

Our *walg*, the water hole we all came from! Fallen fronds are piled up on the rocky bottom. Why has Muruwul dried up? There are no men around to chant for the clouds to come, nor young girls to spill *gulan* ("virgin blood") for the rain to come and wash it away. The hole looks deep and wide now it is empty, or perhaps it is because so many of our souls have swarmed out of it. When I am back in Galwan I must tell Malabin and all my friends what it looks like. That hole the men dug on *nongaru* was much smaller, shallower too. That was good. I slipped

142

inside while I was staring at *dagu*, trying to see the girls lying on the ground behind the screen of withering branches. It was silly of me to worry them. Malabin came back from *dagu* pounding her belly and stamping hard on the ground to loose the stuff the men had left inside. Her skin steamed, and on one of her thighs there was a patch of partly watered blood. I was about to rush toward her, as though there was something painful but magically tempting and sweet that we both ought to share.

"Come on, my *mugul*, you should follow me," a voice whispered behind me. Ranger! The man held a boomerang in his hand, pressing the end of it against my back. I had felt it as soon as the dance started, but it did not dawn on me that the touch meant a signal to follow him to *dagu*.

As the end of the ceremony drew closer and the day drifted toward dusk, the men rubbed our bodies with *yudu* and our own defloration blood. The skin had a slimy touch and a rare sacramental odor, the scent that comes to you only once—in the flowering of your youth—to mark the day when you plunge into life. You are forever seeking to recapture that moment, but it stays beyond your reach.

Above the line of the forest, the clouds from the distant sea gathered in a large flock and rolled forward toward *jangulg* ("the mainland"); the faster ones rushed ahead looking like hands stretched across the sky, reaching Galwan country. Coated with evening red, they had the color of our bodies rubbed with ocher and blood but not the sweating skin and hard breathing the day had known.

My armbands are gone; I must have lost them as I rushed away from nongaru. *Lying without them I look plain and bare, like a featherless cockatoo. It hardly matters to Ranger; he has placed his canvas hat on the greenery to cushion my back. His hand does not quiver and holds no boomerang. Instead of the wood point smeared with* malnar, *fingers touch* maularin *and*

143

thrust inside my dagu *suddenly. No white skin could be called sacred, not in our world after the Wawalags or before. Ranger withdraws his hand, and holding it against his face, licks the bloodstain on his fingers. In the world of the tribe, no girl has been brought to womanhood without the boomerang.*

Along the dry creek bed running into Muruwul, scattered trees shade the ground here and there. Bones feel no pain if they are baked in the sun, but as soon as a man dies, however, the remains should be gathered into a hollow log and taken to the burial cave. Marngit might be back to see that they are properly cared for. Whoever he brings along to help—men or spirits —many hollow logs will be needed. I have already seen several skulls; the other bones . . . I had better watch my step so as not to tread on them.

The track . . . yes, why has it not dawned on me before? The track follows a chain of water holes across the vast, dry plateau of the reserve. The *balandas* must have been along it long ago, carrying with their containers—jars, bags or whatever they carry that stuff in—that make water the last drink you will ever have. When that curse grips you, however eager a man is to run from the place, he can only crawl a shade or two before being pinned to the ground forever. Yes, I must have heard our fellows saying something about that.

The day is heating up fast; I have to sit down for a while. There must be a bush or a boulder to shelter behind. Muru has wandered off along the dry creek bed, searching for a cooler place perhaps. Nothing much here to shield us from the sun; farther along the track maybe. From now on we have to journey at dawn and dusk only; in the cooler air we will breathe easier. It might never rain again in this dry country. Our ancestors must know all about the *balandas* poisoning our water holes and are keeping the rain back for each pool to dry out. The long drought

144

might force the whites to flee back to their own world. Wagudi told me that when the *balandas* grow thirsty they crush the rocks to squeeze out the water. Here they could crush a whole mountain, but only a cloud of dust would come out of it and not a drop of moisture.

Marngit will be back here, surely. The medicine man sees that the bones from the burial cave are finally taken into the sky. You can see the path—the Milky Way stretches across the country and the sea beyond. Our ancestor Boma-Boma paved it from the bones of the dead so as to reach Bralgu and call Djanbuwal to spear the monster, Warngi, that ate part of our land. Later, the sisters traveled along that path, too.

Muru has come back and is clawing me to be followed down to the creek, his snout covered with sand. He must have sensed a frog buried deep in the creek bed. I have to look for *ganinjari* ("stick") to dig with. There will not be much to quench our thirst, but whatever we can squeeze from the frog's belly will be enough to wet our mouths for a day.

CHAPTER SEVEN

There is water down there at the foot of the bluff; half of the pool rests in the shade, darkly mirroring the wall of rock; the other part is brightened by the sun, and the color of each single stone can be clearly seen at the shallow edge of the water. Above hang branches, weighed down by *nara* ("heavy foliage") and bunches of white gum flowers are tucked here and there behind the canopy of green.

Good, I have followed the right track. This morning, while I was walking down from the hill country, I felt that a pool like this would appear. Last night Ure visited me; his voice shook and his eyes drooped. "Both tribes will gather to farewell him—he was a good elder." In spite of the sadness he brought to share with me, good might come of it, I thought. Seeing someone you know, luck could turn your way after all.

Now that the dry stretch of country is behind, I could hurry up. A finger count of camps more and Mount Wawalag will be seen—at last! Yes, I have made it; perhaps even quicker than when I was traveling with Ranger, though when he fled from Galwan he had his "go-pass," that white man's gadget to tell him which way to journey. From here I have to head toward the

146

morning sun; no danger of wandering off route; I know this bush well. Yes, Muru, we both do! You can smell *jiridja*, "our country," too. It's there behind the horizon.

There has to be a cycad palm here; I saw it years ago, with its heavy crop hanging over the water. Yes, it is leaning over the edge of the pool; plenty of fruit on it this season, too. It is a pity the nuts are not to be eaten "raw"; they have to be put in a bag first and left in the water for several days for the bitter juice to come out—otherwise that stuff would rip the guts out of your belly. It is good tucker when it is properly prepared. Both people—Galwan and Narku—pound the nut into flour, wrap a handful of the dough in paperbark and bake it into *ngadu* ("damper"). The palm crop ripens just in time for the beginning of *nara* and is harvested, ready to be pounded on *dugaruru* stone to feed the dancing fellows. The ceremony will be soon; I have made it.

When I was last in Galwan I missed the festivities only by days. It is a pity. It would have been my first *nara*. All of us—Ure, Malabin and Dadangu—looked forward to it. Perhaps everything would have been all right if I had not had to walk to Narku country to fetch Jogu, my younger sister who was staying with our uncle. She had to come and look after *momo*, for after *nara* ceremony I was to go and live with *duwei*.

They could have sent me to Bungul much earlier; many girls go to their *duwei* before their "first bleeding," but maybe I was needed to look after *momo* or perhaps it was because the elders never sat together and talked about me. My *baba* spent most of his time hanging around the *balanda's* hut and had to boil the billy many times each day; he lost all his eyebrows and eyelashes blowing into the fire. *Momo* often said that the white man should go back to his own country, but some of our fellows thought that even if Ranger left, or fell from the cliff into the sea, my father would still have to hang around the *balanda's* hut

147

and boil the billy to serve his soul. Bungul, on the other hand, never went to the *balanda's* hut. He came to Galwan only when the ceremony was to be held, and I began to fear that many seasons would go by before the two men got around to talking about me.

I am glad that someone else thought of it. At Mangrove Swamp the latest of Bungul's wives, Yinguamba, the eldest I think, came to see *momo*, and the two had a long chat. I did not hear everything they were saying, but it was about me, all right. The woman thought that I should move in with them. It was *ngurubilga* ("bad") for a young girl not to be with her *duwei*. Other men might flatter her, and if she ran away with anyone else a fight could break out and people could get hurt. Maybe there was more to it than that; in his hut on the cliff, Ranger told anyone who bothered to listen that each man should have one wife only; he even read it from the book. Perhaps the people thought that he would persuade my father to flog me off to someone else, or even find a *balanda* for me.

Mother must have felt the same way. "You should go soon. I will come to goanna country [she always used the totem of the people instead of the tribal name] and show you how to make those crab traps."

"The other two women will know. They will teach me."

"You have to be good and fast. It's a big *babaru* ["family"]. There will be many mouths to feed, and they're growing old, all of them."

On the way to Mangrove Bay we met Bungul with a group of Narku men rushing up the Wawalag slopes and heading toward the Gunga River on the other side of the mountain; they were in too much of a hurry to tell us what had happened. Warinji, the last in the group, stopped and waved his spear: "Ranger, the *balanda*, has blown up the sisters!"

We went on toward Mangrove Bay, *momo* stopping now and

148

then as if she wanted to say something, but instead she struggled with her thoughts and waving her free hand mumbled, "They should get him; that man will rip up the whole country."

Much later, when we stopped for a break and sat down in the shade of a banyan tree, she told me about schooner people, the first *balandas* with sunburned skin and faces hardened by salt winds. They came from the far sea during the Dry and wandered along the coast. They would land on the shore in their dinghies but never stayed for long, took away no rocks and never poisoned the water holes. That happened long ago, even before *momo* was born, during the lives of her grandmothers. I have seen a schooner that Gunbuna drew in lines of white clay on a big sheet of bark smeared with red ocher. The boat looked different from the barge; it had a tall mast that stretched up like the trunk of a lone tree. There were several men on board and behind them perched a fowl, which was taken on the sea to give them eggs. No one told me why our men painted a picture of the schooner once a year and why they put the bark sheet where everyone could see it; not only Galwan but even the people from inland *malas* and tribes along the coast as far as the sun reaches before it sits down.

They say the schooners brought the first steel ax to the black man, long before Doctor Cross came, and they gave our men tobacco. The old people thought the newcomers were good so long as they stayed on their boats, but one of the sailers got ashore and wandered through the bush, sneaking deep inland, past the Wawalag Rocks and down the Upper Valley to tread on *nongaru* when our elders were building the "women's shade" and preparing for the ceremony. So many spears flew that when he was hit, the man did not fall down but stayed propped up on the shafts. His bones were later put in a hollow log, the same as every black fellows, and then taken over Mount Wawalag and right down to the last point of the peninsula to a craggy cape

149

looming over the mouth of Mangrove Bay. The bones were put in a small cave for the *balandas* to come and collect them, but the schooner never sailed in again. The log has since rotted away, but the bones are still there, our fellows say.

There were other boats, different from schooners, that called in, too. *Momo's* mother remembered them, I was told. The people saw the boats through the calm early morning air, sneaking between the northern tip of the peninsula and Durana Island, only during the Dry. Wherever they went a column of smoke rose up in the air like a willy-willy, and it always appeared before anything else was seen. Perhaps the boats showed the smoke to pretend they were on fire so that they could come close to the shore to seek help. The *balandas* often do that to show they are a harmless lot. The boats used to come right against Red Cliff for the men to come ashore. Wherever they did so, the *balandas* grabbed the people, mostly the young, chained them up and led them into the belly of the ship. No one ever learned why the people were taken away or where. The chained ones never came back to tell, and it looked as though the sea had swallowed the ship and all those on it as well.

From the plain below the bluffs the breeze brings the smell of the sea from the far horizon. It feels now as if I am sitting on the Wawalag slopes, looking down on *nara* lagoon. Will Malabin know I am heading back? Ure might have told her and she will pass it on to . . . no, I doubt if she will be bothered with that while she is mourning. My *duwei,* my man is dead! Yes, he is. The message stick must have gone through the country to take the sad news to every tribal soul. His *babaru* will gather, relatives too, the men to chant and the women . . . their wailing will veil the country like an unseen cloud laden with pain and sorrow. The voices of Yinguamba and Djulgu will be the loudest. What a pity I have not been told the right words or I too could wail from here.

150

When an elder departs the country mourns too, for trees have souls just as humans do. Many of the branches might keep still today, and many of them will droop their leaves. Narku country is larger than the eyes can see, stretching from Mount Wawalag toward the setting sun and following the coast where it passes Balanda Cape—a rocky stretch of land that rises from the sea like an immense *dugong* that has come out of the water to plunge its head into the peninsula. From the Cape, the sea swings around and sneaks deep inland to flank the Wawalag's mountain from behind, so forming Mangrove Bay. However, in spite of all the force of the tide rushing in to flood the mangrove forest and in spite of all those waves that day and night pass the Balanda Rock and enter the bay, the sea makes no impression on the mountain. A good stretch of land is left between the Wawalags and the bay. Most of it is covered with mangrove swamps where the Narku people, the goanna worshippers, gathered, for food is not hard to come by near the water and the dense forest.

There is no need to follow the coast when you are going to Narku country. Even a beast would run out of breath going that way; there is a much shorter track, "over the neck" *momo* called it. It leads from Pandanus Springs, over the cliffs to avoid the Upper Valley so that we women do not tread on *nongaru*, and then moves from the rocky slopes down again to follow the path of Malgu River and right down the top end of Mangrove Bay.

My uncle and his *babaru* often camped near the mouth of the river, just at the edge of the mangrove forest. It is a good one-camp journey even for the men, and they have to hit the track before the first sun. When we were on our way there, *momo* and I had to break our journey and camp. There is a banyan tree right on the track near the river with an immense trunk and a mass of roots hanging down from the lower part of the tree that makes a shelter better than any man-built hut. We

151

always stopped there for the night, lit the fire and then gathered food from the bush—even if there was nothing better than yams; the ground around always seemed full of them.

I had better come out of the pool. Muru has brought a large bird, a duck by the look of it. He has put the catch down on the ground at the edge of the water and sits by it waiting for me to come out and do something. I will have to make a fire and see that we both have a good meal. It is a nice place. I would not mind staying here for several days, but Galwan lures me on. Ranger called this place a "bloody good dam." I did not know the white man's lingo then and did not grasp what he meant. Even if I had known *balanda* words, I would have been too scared to speak, even to cry out for help or to squeal, as helpless animals do when they are trapped.

A cry and struggle could have helped perhaps; it never occurred to me then. I had been dumb ever since that day when *momo* and I were camped behind the banyan tree and before I could even see Ranger properly, my arms were twisted behind my back. *Momo* senses what was happening much quicker than I did and swung her leading stick and screamed. I am not sure whether she hit him, but she got me for sure, right on top of the head; a lump like an emu egg grew there.

I had to follow the man. What else can a girl do when one of her arms is handcuffed to a *balanda's* wrist? Ranger ran through the bush fast, along the edge of the mangrove forest, giving me no time to see where I was going. A splinter of wood got stuck between two toes and went a good way into my foot. Whenever I bent and tried to pull it out, the metal ring around my wrist dragged me forward. In his free hand Ranger held a gun and swung around with it to move the branches out of his way. Not that he was afraid of the bush, but the fellows were on his heels; not only Narku men but Galwan fellows as well.

They nearly got him just the other side of Malgu River. He was climbing up the bank when a spear was thrown, but it only

152

brushed the top of his head. He stepped back and then forced me forward. A short distance away. Warinji dashed out from behind a bush, his spear above his head, ready to be launched from the thrower; then he paused, staring at me. A trail of flame burst from behind my back and, the next moment Warinji was not there. The spear came to rest in the bush with the shaft swaying, the stone blade sticking up. Below the spear the blood-stained leaves rustled.

I will have to find some mud near the pool and roll the duck in it to cover all the feathers. It does not take long to cook a bird. You bury it in the hot ashes and wait for a while. Then, when the mud around it becomes stone-hard, you pull it out and knock off the chunks of burned clay; all the feathers come off, too. I have to watch what food I take now. A mother-to-be should not eat kangaroo joeys, nor young chicks. Fowl and turtle eggs can cause harm too. I must stay away from the young offspring of any animal. A small lump shows on my belly, but it should grow fast. I had made a little spear, less than a hand span long, and carry it around in my bag; that is how you ask for a boy. They say my mother waved a tiny basket to tell the spirits she wished for a girl. When I was last here with Ranger we did not light a fire in any camp before this one. He was afraid the line of smoke would give him away. The men were after him all over the country, and at the end of each day he crawled into a bush like a possum or anteater and dragged me on top of him to shield his body if the spears came. He was always on the lookout for a trench dug by a creek so that when he stretched out to rest I would have to lie on top of him and not slide off because of the bank. Even if I did slip off during the night, my wrist was locked to his and I could not move far away.

Here, just in this patch, he dug a large hole in the soft ground to lie in, but the sand slipped off the banks whenever one of us moved and he kept spitting it out of his mouth. The sand drove him mad; he swore at it and then got up and moved to that tree over there with a big hollow trunk. It would have been just wide enough for him to fit his back inside if he had not had the rucksack; the bag was not so much big as heavy and full of rocks. Even when he slept, Ranger kept his rucksack on, with the stones in it pressing against his body, perhaps to make sure the load was close to him. He took it off only now and then during the daytime when we stopped for him to make love. Even then he kept staring at them, and his eyes seldom rested on me.

Something has closed in my chest, in my throat too. My jaws feel stiff; I cannot swallow any food. Muru might like it; here—a whole bird for you. Go on, furry, you haven't eaten for days; last night your belly rumbled—it's hunger thunder, they say. There are several more camps to journey, you know. You don't get far on an empty belly, whether you travel on two legs or four. That food might be too hot; let it cool down for a while.

Why as B . . . no, it is *ngurubilga* to mention the name of your dead husband. Why did he die? Ure said nothing about it. Perhaps a snake bit him? A man could slip on wet sea rocks and break his skull, fall from a tree . . . so much could happen. Whatever curse strikes, it comes because the spirits want it that way and for reasons often known to them but not to us. Yes, I felt something was about to happen in our country when Marngit left in a hurry, leaving me at Muruwul water hole days ago. He must have pleaded with the spirits to save poor *duwei*, for he was his half brother. Yes, *duwei* was getting old, but not so much as others. Think of Gunbuna, Wagudi and scores of others—all his seniors.

Would Ranger know that *duwei* has gone? Marngit or another of our fellows might have appeared in his dreams to bring the news. The *balanda* might know all about that already; his mob seems to be pretty well informed about what is happening in our world.

154

CHAPTER EIGHT

The sun has gone mad today; it has raced as never before, cutting down the shade of the trees into mere patches and now, high above, it looks like a red-hot stone tossed up into the sky. It has a long way to go yet, but in the evening when it sets the sea around will boil.

If it had not been for Gururgu Crossing, I could rest in the shade now, waiting for the cooler part of the day to journey in, but the river should be just near here. I have been hoping to camp on it since morning; it should appear soon. Once it does I will make camp, have a good spell . . . cross Gururgu at first light just to be safe. I doubt if the whites will be around to set traps, but the old men are wise, and when they tell you something, especially in a dream, you had better stick to it if you want to save your head. Ure listened to them; he must have gone through here long ago.

I wonder whether the elders mind me coming back to the country now that my *duwei* is dead. The men do not change their minds very often; even when they decide something wrongly, they still like to hold to their word. Normally I would have to go to Ure, like Yinguamba and Djulgu will do; according to the custom, he has to care for all of us from now on. I am not so sure about me, however; the fact that I was taken away could cause some trouble. Still, I am Ure's brother's *galei* ("woman"). If he does not want me, what am I to do then?

Ure knows I did not live with Ranger when I was in town; I doubt if any of us would. He might have a woman of his own color, but if he does she must be made of rock. Ranger could knock a stone chip off her now and then and that would make him the happiest husband in the country; and . . . yes, wherever he goes he could carry her on his back instead of a rucksack. That bag seemed as heavy as a boulder, and he would not part with it. Perhaps our fellows would not have caught up with him if he had less on his shoulders. Worn out by his journey, he slept so soundly that he saw the fellows only after they had pushed me from on top of him and Ure held *gara* ("spear blade") against his throat. Our fellows know how to track during the dark well; it is like chasing an animal. When the worn-out beast sleeps, you can creep up to it without fear of being heard.

A line of mud banks, dry and hard, stretches along the edge of the paperbark forest, making a sharp cut between the dark surface of the ground and the light color of the tree trunks. No, it is not Goromuru; the river has a sandy floor with heaps of pebbles piled up here and there where the water has wandered from its course and elbowed its way into the banks. It floods during the Wet, stacking heaps of branches, fronds and clumps of dead grass against the tree trunks so that you can see how high the torrent has reached.

I must be on the right track. Muru is leading the way, and he would not go anywhere else but Galwan. Perhaps we have wandered off course . . . yes, it is a swamp we are making our way across. The paperbark trees do not look so happy; the leaves—half of them are gone and the rest have turned

156

yellow—and the plants look a sad lot, not a twig or flower to be seen. The water from the swamp has gone, taking with it the lilies and *ragai* ("bullrushes"); it seems that there are not even any mosquitoes left. There is hardly anything for a *babaru* to live on if the people have to hang around for long.

No place is kinder to man than Mangrove Bay. There are enough crabs and oysters there for every black soul, and if you cross the narrow tail of the peninsula, you can gather piles of turtle eggs from the beaches facing the open sea. Ure will take me; how could it be otherwise? A woman does not go back to her *babaru*, and I doubt if she could live on her own. She is to be with her *duwei* until death, and if he goes first, she will be taken over by his brother or closest relative. The elders know exactly who is in line to care for her. It is not they who made that law, but they were told how life is to be by the Wawalags.

I am not sure if you should believe all the men say; the Wawalags had no husbands to care for and listen to, yet they bred children and made all the ceremonies. They even made rain. I am not saying the elders are wrong, but men are made differently and like to feel they are the boss—black and white alike. That fellow, Jesus or Justice, wants every man to have only one woman, but that would be even worse. With only one pair of hands you would have to gather yams, search for crabs, keep the fire, and I was promised to my *duwei* to care for him since all of them will grow old. A head can have more than one of us to gather food, keep the fire and raise children. He can make love to any of us when he feels like it; that is how the Wawalags told us to be and it was good that they did. When a man has one or more of us at his camp to sleep with, he will not chase any other women and will steer clear of trouble. The whites can call us "women" or "wives," whatever pleases them; we are just a family.

Come on, my furry friend, keep going. The river will come

157

soon. The bottom of the swamp has crusted over, a dry claypan gripped by drought. The ground reminds me of an old face I have seen somewhere. When you turn around, the place looks somehow empty, as though a monster has swept down from the sky, scraped up a huge chunk of the country and left the bush to struggle with its wound. When I was last here the place looked much happier; it was the end of the Dry, like now, but water lay under the shade of the paperbark trees, partly covered with lily leaves. The flower season was just about past its best then, though the birds still hung around drawing out nectar with their long beaks. In Galwan, I think, they call the anther of the flower head *maularin*, the same as a part of the woman's vagina. Near the edge of the water, Ranger found some crocodile eggs; you do not need many of them for a meal. At one place we had to cut across an arm of the swamp and struggle through waist-deep water. I could not help asking myself what would happen to me if the crocodile got Ranger, the beast has strong teeth and powerful jaws, but I doubt if he could have ripped off the handcuffs; even our fellows were helpless against them.

Our men had to cut off Ranger's hand to free me, but I was left with a pair of rings on my wrist, jangling all the time and splashed all over with blood. White man's blood is red, just like ours; it felt warm on my skin, and a patch of it somehow even got on my lips . . . it tasted terribly salty. The fellows felt strange, too. When you hunt an animal, you finish it as soon as there is a moment to plunge in the spear, but that does not happen with a man. Our men gathered together—my father, *duwei*, Wagudi, Dadangu, Ure and many others—to talk over what to do.

"The whites will come to look for him," worried my father.

"Let them meet the spears. It's our country," said Bungul.

"It'll be turned into dust and sand. They'll come in flocks."

"We've driven off *balandas* before."

They sat in a circle on the dusty ground and looked as though they were not in a hurry; perhaps it was not easy for them to

158

make up their minds. In our life before, everything was done the way Wawalags advised the men in their dreams, and they would do nothing else. Perhaps the women had never said a single word about *balandas* and how one should deal with them. When something new crops up in life the elders often take their time and wait for the Wawalags to appear in their dreams and tell the men what they should do. Otherwise, the spirits from Bralgu could send word to Marngit and the medicine man will then come and pass it on to the elders.

"No *balanda* shall tread on our land unduly; we have been told that," remembered Bungul.

" '. . . Nor should black man raise his spear in anger,' " reminded my father.

"Finish him with *barlait* ["club"] then. It's your job."

My father and *duwei* had begun to argue; I could not hear them properly, but I reckon it was all about who should spear Ranger. It looked as though neither of the two men was very keen on the job, and they had to talk to find out who is obliged by custom to do it. It looked . . . yes, *duwei* thought that father had flogged me to the *balanda* in return for a packet of tobacco and a steel knife and so broke the promise made when I was born about who should be my rightful man. That upset father; he stood up, shouted a few words and left. With him went all *jiridja* men, without having decided anything.

It was left to *duwei* to do the thinking, and it looked as though he was neither quick nor good at it. He and the other *dua* men talked for a while and then stood up and left. I began to follow them, keeping a good distance behind. *Duwei* did not like it. He shouted something back that sounded like "*dagu win*" ("long vagina").

It is quite a swear word, but I pretended I had heard nothing. Then he yelled again, "Go to your bloody Boma-Boma, you raper."

How long is it since Ure passed through here; it is hard to tell.

159

He walked off the dry claypan over that bank, leaving behind some disturbed sand. There has been no wind since, for it would have wiped away the footprints. He must have been feeling well; they were long steps in a straight line across the soft ground. Fool, he has forgotten to drag a branch behind him. Journeying for so long makes you feel safe, but you ought to keep your mind on it. "*Balandas* always sleep with one eye open." Was it Wagudi or Gunbuna I heard that from?

Gururgu should be near now. The ground is sandy and there are many pebbles scattered about, all smooth after their long journey. The hills where the stones have come from stretch toward the horizon, but there is one boulder sticking above the scrub, hardly a voice ahead of me. Farther down from it you can see the great snake of the river making a pathway toward the sea. I had better stop and camp at the boulder. No fire can be lit because the smoke will give me away; it reaches farther than the eyes and the voice ever can.

I wonder if there are any flies hanging around the place; only they and the animals can sense if humans have been there lately. It was lucky for Ranger I went back. A whole swarm of flies were around him, and it looked as though the insects meant to finish him off. I took a branch and sat down, fighting them back whenever they buzzed about. His arm looked bad at first, but it got a bit better later, and there was nothing left to do but wait for the wound to heal. I rubbed it with *dalhu*, "a green stem full of juice," the kind the elders use when they paint pictures and rub the stem over the surface to set the colors. *Momo* used it for skin cuts and mosquito bites. Ranger did not like the grass tickling his wounds; it hurt. I had to squeeze out the juice first and gently rub his arm with it. Days later, when the new skin grew, I found some goanna fat. It stops the skin from itching and heals the wound much quicker.

A clump of *muwaga* vines creep around one side of the

160

boulder; I have seen hardly any yams here, and this one seems to grow better for being away from the crowded scrub. Muru lifts his leg against the bush and throws some sand on it with his back paws.

Yes, Ure has camped here, shielded by the boulder. He had a large *muwaga*, nipped off the stem and ate the rest. He must have felt too tired to throw that wasted piece away in the bush or bury it in the sand. After many moons on a journey the limbs grow numb; the mind, too. Muru still sniffs that vine, trying to wet on it though there is nothing left to squirt. The dog—he must sense something—he has never carried on like this before. There will still be some yams in the ground. No, it is safer to have nothing and go to sleep. The chill of dawn will wake me up when the boulders are cool.

The dawn is nearly over. The red tide sweeps across the sky, and it will not be long before the sun shows. The day has beaten me to the river. I hoped the early birds would wake me, but I did not hear them. Muru slept like a fallen log, too.

Watch your step; the whites are cunningly clever when they set traps. Ure did not care about it much; he stopped over there to empty his belly. A mess like that should be buried or it casts a smell and gathers flies, all of which can give you away. The elders would not like to see any of us traveling like that; even a fool could track you.

The Wawalags will be seen soon. Yes, Muru, wait until the morning air clears a bit; our country will show up. You know why that mountain is there. Come on, furry friend, surely you know! How would we know where to go back to without it? That mountain can be seen from the edge of the horizon by every soul stranded in the bush. Do not lag behind, I have to trail a branch behind you. Foolish Ure; he did not wipe his marks away. Look, his steps have shortened; the footprints do not lie in

161

a straight line anymore. He swayed while he was walking. There, he stopped again. A nasty running belly that must have been. Poor fellow, you can tell how man feels by the marks he leaves behind.

I know now why Ranger refused to eat yams. Yes, he must have feared that some *balandas* might have been through the bush setting baits; he touched neither roots nor stems. Eggs were the only food he ate. I was hoping he would come to a river where I could get a fish or crabs and show him how good I was at gathering them; but we did not make it together so far. When I woke one morning he was not there any longer and the rocks had gone, too. I felt sure that the town would not be far away; perhaps he wanted to show the other whites that he had crossed the whole reserve on his own.

Keep on, my furry friend. No *balanda* could trick you. I, too, felt something was strange about that *muwaga* vine; you can never tell what the whites might be up to. They can mess up our food, just as they do with the water. It's lucky you warned me.

The bush fire has swept through Gururgu Crossing. When I was last here, vines and bushes hid the riverbanks, and high above them tall trees reached out in a green canopy to bridge the blue mat of the sky. Hardly more than a handful of charcoal is left now; the wind has blown away the ashes, leaving behind soot-caked stones. Not a bird is to be seen. The river, too, seems to have been frightened off, and the hunted reptiles have sunk under the sand, waiting to sneak safely away.

Ure sat on that patch of sand and left his spear. Poor soul, no man travels without his tool. I will take it with me; the shaft feels so smooth from the grip of his hand. I had better climb up the bank and press on with the journey; from Gururgu toward the rising sun stretches the Galwan country, and I know most of it. There is a valley with tall trees about a camp's walk from here with *birgurda* ("bees") nesting in a hollow log. I could stay

162

there and have a rest; the spell would do me good, and Muru too; he is worn out, and we do not have to hurry now. The Wet should have begun already, but luckily the rain is late this season; it looks as though it will not be here for a while yet. Maybe Djanbuwal is taking the rain somewhere else, or perhaps our fellows have not got around to making the ceremonies. The Wet cannot begin before *nara*, and the ceremony will not be held for a while.

Children are seldom born during the monsoon, but by the time the rain comes it might be over. The lump in my belly is getting bigger; I like to hold my palm over it and gently tickle the skin. I cannot feel anything inside; the boy has not learned to kick yet, and he might not cry much when he comes either. If the monsoon begins, the Wet should not bother me. During the rains, food is easier to come by; Yinguamba and Djulgu might help me make the hut. They will be weaving a mat for me, I feel sure. The spirits always let your relatives know when you are on the way home.

Should I call the boy *Urban* "emu"; I dreamed of the bird last night, and it looked huge, much bigger than the one I saw up in the stone country painted on that rock shelter. It ran in front of me, plunging its claws into the dust. It stopped now and then to wallow for a while in the dust and before it took off again, it left behind a big egg for me.

PART THREE

CHAPTER ONE

They have stripped the top off the mountain. All the trees, scrub, even the mosses have been scraped off, leaving behind the bare rock. From a distance it looks like a bald head, but when it is seen from a voice away it is a sky-high boulder. The rocks have been knocked about to give the mountain a new shape—one to please the *balandas* but not the one the spirits planned.

Momo must know what has happened to our country but she will say nothing. She quivers, her head hangs (her neck is too weak to hold it up), and even if by some magic she could form a word or two, her body will lack the strength to sound them out. I should cuddle the poor soul. Luckily I found her; what a pity we cannot talk—there is so much to ask and tell.

A noise is suddenly heard, rattling against the bare bluffs and echoing over the bulldozed bush. With it comes a helicopter, which hovers above piles of uprooted trees, preparing to land on a small rise. Through the glass two heads are seen inside. No, they could not have noticed me; I have been quick to dash under the tangled branches of the nearest pile. I can see the machine

167

wallowing in the dust as it touches the ground.

What are the *balandas* up to? I can feel *momo*'s heart beating under my hand. It stops for a moment and . . . here it comes again, pounding like a beak. We all have to struggle to breathe, whatever shape they make us into. I found her this morning, floating in a trough of oil down at the building site. Poor old thing! Yes, it must be *momo*; the bird would shy away if it was not she.

Both *balandas* have alighted from the machine, though I can see only one of them. He looks over the cleared bush toward the mountain. "This is chiefly groundwork for the new township. Up there we have to get rid of some nasty hanging rocks. We can't let them loom over our backyard. Look at them, so enormous—nature has been really generous here."

The Wawalags are still on the summit, but they look different now and it is hard to tell one sister from another. The younger one, Garangal, I think, has been cut off to her waist. Now she looks like the stump of a tree. The other sister, Boaliri—they spared her height but fiddled with her shape; where her hips had been there is now a wall of freshly crushed rocks. A pair of breasts, only showing toward the horizon, sagging like most of our mothers' were, are gone too, leaving behind pale patches to mark the spot where the rocks had been blasted off.

"You've made such progress here, the corporation must be very pleased. Your father would have been proud of you, too." I can see only part of her through the bushes.

"Luck is on our side—the world has become hungry for uranium again." He wears a white shirt; I can see both sleeves, though one must be empty.

Momo scratches my skin. Cockatoos rarely show their tough claws. Ranger has upset her; even as a bird she hates his voice. I found her late yesterday. She was heading toward Boma-Boma Cape when the whites blasted the top of the mountain. I cannot

168

feel any wound under the feathers; perhaps it was fright that brought her down. What a big blast. The mountain trembled like a wounded snake and coughed out a huge cloud of dust and earth! The cloud rose up, blotted out the sun perching on the sea far away, and the sky turned a somber red, as though the blood of the earth, or perhaps that of the Wawalags, had gushed out with the rocks, to fly sky high and then come splattering down over the lower slopes and settle into dust.

"Yesterday as I flew in I looked for that hut your father built when he first came here."

Ranger turns away from the mountain. "It used to be at Red Cliff, far down at the river mouth. The whole area is under excavation. I'd like you to see the blasting down there; it should take place soon."

"There's so much dust around." Why has she come to see him? Wuluru moves to get a better view of Gunga Valley. I doubt whether she has been here before, though Cross must have told her all about our country.

"There's enough uranium in that valley to feed the world for decades. It'll be dusty work digging that out. The blasting shouldn't take long."

If she had been here yesterday, Wuluru could have seen them blast the mountain. What a blast; the cloud of dust changed from red to black and then drifted away, hovering for a while above the peninsula. As the summit came back into view the men could be seen walking out of their hideouts, and the metallic noise of the steel tools bounced and rattled against the rocks. The sound stayed in the air long after the shape of the hills had sunk into darkness. It sounded strange and ugly, as though someone had come from a far country, lassoed the peninsula with a steel rope and forced the earth, like a trapped animal, into an immense cage.

I hope the *balandas* will go soon; it feels very cramped hiding

169

under the branches. I'd better not lean on *momo* or she will shriek. Her feathers still feel damp. It might take a while for the oil to dry; the greasy stuff is not so easily taken off the feathers as the birds do it with water. There is always a breeze up there at Cape Boma-Boma—that might help. Yes, that is where *momo* wants to be taken. How long before the spirits from Bralgu come to fetch her? You do not journey there through the sky any longer as they did in the old days. A ferryman comes now to take you safely across the sea. It might be better that way; many old souls could never make that trip on their own.

"That island farther north—it's Durana, I presume?"

"Yes. Bralgu is supposedly farther on—it's a mythical island anyway."

He never believed our world is there and that the tribal ancestors will someday return to the mainland. Wait until Djanbuwal appears in the sky; he will make him believe. Yes, that ancestor must come. When you get there, *momo*, do hurry him. The *balandas* will grind the country into dust if he is not here soon.

"There's a cliff from which their ferryman used to sail off for the Land of the Dead, with tribal souls in his canoe."

"You mean Cape Boma-Boma. See those sea rocks farther up the coast beyond the building site? Not one of those ferried blacks ever came back," he sneers. "No sign of that blast yet!"

Boma-Boma did come; the ancestors sent him here to guard the country from malevolent spirits. The Wawalags waited for him down at the shore, made a camp and baked *ngadu*, "damper from cycad nut." That night he slept with both Wawalags and broke his back while making love.

What a pity there is no ancestor to guard the country now. From the small plateau at Marain Cave right down to the shore of Warngi Inlet, there is not a single tree or bush to be seen; nothing but piles of stumps, topsoil and crushed branches. At

170

dusk the man-made hillocks look like *warngi*, the "monsters that come out of the sea." *Momo* will tell the ancestors in Bralgu what the whites are up to here. Wait until Djanbuwal hears all about the scarred land.

"That hotel looks very impressive." Wuluru must be looking at the cluster of new buildings near Warngi Inlet, at the foot of the mountain. One of them is built of boulders; that would be the hotel. I looked at it from a distance yesterday and wondered why the walls do not fall down; the boulders have no flat sides and do not rest easily on each other. They are all right sitting in the sea where the sand is soft and they can sink halfway into the ground. They were scattered all over Warngi Inlet—the eggs of that monster that tried to come to shore—but they all went bad and never hatched. Some of them showed above the sea all the time, others only at low tide, when the water is so shallow that it hardly comes up to your navel.

Momo preens her damp feathers. That sludge must taste awful; her whole beak is covered in muck. Birds cannot spit to clean their mouths; I wish there were some seeds about, to take her mind off the oily taste. Cockatoos will eat green grass of young shoots, though there is none here. They raise their young on *munji* ("wild berries") and often search the bush for nuts as well.

"Have you heard anything about Marngit?" Why does she want to know about him?

"I doubt he'll be around, unless he can live on dust."

I wish I could slip away down to the shore and look for some seaweed if nothing else is to be found. Muru, the dog, must be down on the shore sniffing about for some food. Yesterday he found a dead fish washed up on the beach. Those sea rocks from which the *balandas* made the walls were always covered with oysters, and it was easy to fill your belly if you knew how to open the shells. The Galwan people often gathered at the bay; I used

171

to be able to tell the rock where each one sat snoozing in the sun and waiting for their bellies to be ready for another meal, but it would be hard to recognize the boulders now. They look quite different in the wall—the shells have gone, even the layer of lichen has been scraped off and the surface washed with some magic stuff so that you can only see shiny specks glittering in the sun here and there.

Momo is still troubled by the sludge; what about something to get her mind off that stuff? There must be a grain or two of seed among the uprooted trees here. A gum nut over there . . . hold on. I stretched clumsily, and a dry branch under me snapped. The *balandas* might have heard it.

"Actually, we're short of a tribesman, one with some sense. Only his shadow can be seen now."

"What about that lad—didn't your late father suggest him?"

"We'd rather have a full-blood. Our P.R. people wouldn't like the idea of having an outsider. He's a descendant of the mother's line only. That excludes him from inheriting the land under tribal custom."

They must be talking about Plonk. That bloody canvas hat —why does he have to wear it?

"So you have a whole country full of uranium and are short of a traditional owner?" I hear sand squeaking under her shoes.

"We leased the land from the Crown. The blacks aren't entitled to it. However, since they were the traditional owners, I suggested to the corporation that we get some sort of deal with them as well." His voice sounded hollow.

The sand squeaks louder now. Perhaps they are about to catch me, but they keep chatting as though nothing is happening. *Momo* quivers; she holds on to me with both claws. Hold on, you poor thing. They're not after us, we'll just hide under our trees. Though uprooted and tangled, the trees are ours. This scarred, bare land—it is ours, too. Here, look through this gap

172

between the branches. See Warngi Inlet; it's a pity we're not down there now. Do you remember all those people who used to gather at the shore?

Ranger leans on a log sticking out of the pile. "They're certainly running late with that blast today."

"That island, Durana . . ."

He interrupts. "It used to be the detention center; it's still restricted."

"I hope I'll be moving there soon. Your father did explain how ideal that island would be for our center. It lies halfway between the mainland and Bralgu. We wouldn't need to build an enclosure there."

His voice turns dry. "It's not possible, I'm afraid."

My limbs have grown numb. I hope the *balandas* will go away soon. I should be careful not to harm Urban lying like this. Here he is; feel him, *momo*. Just press your head against my belly. His totem will be the emu bird like you, though the emu never flies.

"I thought your corporation would have no objection if the center moves to Durana. Your father discussed it with you. We have been talking of this for years."

"I'm only in charge of the field operation. The decisions are made by H.Q. What's happened to that blast?"

When Ranger is upset, he moves around; he will be doing it shortly. I can tell by his voice.

"Had there been any arrangement between the corporation and your father? I am entitled to know."

A shadow of the shirt sleeve flattened by the breeze dances on the stump of an uprooted tree. "The situation suited him and us. The corporation will sponsor the program only so long as the blacks are kept away from this area."

As soon as they move away I shall dash out. There are many piles of dead trees down the slope to shelter me from the

173

balandas' view, but I will have to be very fast.

"You shouldn't have let the blacks out of the center." The shadow of the empty sleeve has moved away.

"I understood we were to move to that island, so I let them go. There's about eight hundred kilometers of bush between the town and us. No one will cross that, certainly not in the condition they're in."

"Haven't you heard of blacks crossing the Western Desert? They do it in no time. I have to be sure they get back in that enclosure. That blast . . . I have to radio and see what happened." He walks back to the helicopter.

Hold on, *momo,* your oily feathers could easily slip from my hand while I run. Cling to my skin, come on; cockatoos have strong claws. Hold on, little thing, do not slip out of my hands. There are no *balandas* in Bralgu; the white man will never get there. Maybe it is much safer to be off. Most of our people must have headed that way. The country is not much of a place to stay in now, even for *djabari* ("scorpion"). There is not very far to go. Look, there is a long trench dug across the slopes; let us dash in.

The land trembles—poor soul, our country.

Something is heard from the mountaintop. It could not be that helicopter; the noise is coming from the ground. Perhaps the land is about to vomit. It does indeed: some of the rocks have come down from the summit and, rolling toward the sea, fly over the trench.

Hold on, *momo,* it will not be long now. Look, I can see Cape Boma-Boma already, and farther beyond is Durana Island— the floating carcass of that sea monster. I doubt if the whites will go there too; the Wawalags and us, that is who the *balandas* are after. *Momo,* did that Warngi monster have white skin? It came from the far sea, like them; it must have been that color. I hope you'll find some seeds if the ferryman does not turn up soon.

Many of our people are on the way to Bralgu and he could be quite busy. "No tribal soul is forgotten." You told me that, I remember. I'll call here in a few days to bring you some food if you have to wait for him. Muru will help me find some; he sniffs around at night. There ought to be a rubbish dump somewhere, and who can tell that better than an old dingo.

A thick cloud of dust from Gunga Valley has shrouded the country. Its fringes look red, inflamed by the evening sun. Perhaps it is blood. Yes, *momo*, you told me once: "When it is ripped, the land bleeds just like a mother." I doubt we'll find any seeds for you. Warngi Inlet looks a strange place now, not ours any longer. Yesterday I walked along the beach to look for those pools under the paperbark trees. You would never have gone hungry at this place before. If you did not get a good catch of fish or crabs, there would always be duck or reptile eggs hidden in the sand and bushes. I could not find even a single pool, and I had to wander around all day long. There was not a bush, tree or rock that would tell me the right way. It was Warngi Inlet, all right, with the waves washing the shore, but the land all around looked shorn and dug out. I hoped that at least there would be holes left in the ground that would mark the spot where the pools had once been. The yams had gone, too. I had a long, sharp stone with a pointed end that you plunge into the ground, but it brought me nothing but an occasional chunk of tree root, long dead but unable to rot in the dry sand.

Here, *momo*, rest on this rock. The evening breeze will dry you fast. You can preen while you wait; the ferryman should not be long. Come and see us often. Urban will be born soon; I shall tell him all about you. Do visit our dreams, *momo*; yes, come tonight and tell us all that has happened to our people. You know, I did see those other girls from *nongaru*—a whole flock of them, pink-breasted and pretty. I'll tell you all about them when you come to see me at night—please do. Did I tell you Djan-

175

buwal struck that dreadful old man with *larban*. Yes, he did.

The earth, like a wounded beast, rumbled all night. In the dark it was hard to tell whether it was *balandas* crushing the rocks or Djanbuwal summoning the clouds.

Luckily I found a shelter for the night. Sometime ago, when they blew off one of Balari's breasts, it rolled down from the summit toward the bay, knocked into a bulldozer and split into two pieces. It is a huge boulder, but the higher the rock the better the shelter; when it is warmed by the sun it keeps its heat during the night. I had to squeeze between the rock and the ground and scratch out some soil to make a nest. Tracks wound nearby to the top of the mountain. Nothing bothered me during the night, but now . . . I should have left at dawn and not let myself be caught in the daylight out in the open. A car has just moved off the track and the machine whines, struggling over the rough ground toward the boulder. I had better dash out quickly and hide behind the wreck. A part of the bulldozer, a blade by the look of it, has been thrown off and tossed some distance away, plunging sideways into the ground; it should do for a shelter.

They must be surveyors, with their white pegs that they stick all over the cleared bush. A peg put near here might become *marain* to them, for it will mark the place where the machine stood up to the boulder. There is not much left of it, only a heap of steel half buried in the ground. This oily patch just below the wreck is like a dark shadow covering the dust; the beast has lost its guts.

"This is Juliatown, rising out of the virgin bush."

It is that spotty girl with the notebook and camera. She does not hold a pencil now but speaks into a microphone.

"The place is named after a native girl, given, presumably, by tribesmen to a local ranger who later discovered uranium here. It was their token tribute to his endeavor. It is believed she led

176

him to the find."

She holds something in her hand—a dry stump or a water bag? It is hard to tell as it is partly hidden behind her back. "Over that escarpment, up there behind me, is a Marain Cave. We were asked not to film there; it's the traditional tribal burial place. No strangers are allowed near it. The first curator was appointed to the caves recently, a man formerly a member of Doctor Cross's staff. Doctor Cross's last wish was to be buried there among his adopted black brothers. However, that will have to wait for a while until this hectic development subsides."

Far away, in the direction of Bralgu where the rim of the sky rests on the misty water, a cloud has risen. It looks like the immense head of a bearded old man who has sprung up a few spears high from the sea to have a good look at the land. Two dark spots mark the hollows of the eyes and the mouth seems to be wide open, like the mouths of men when they chant; long tufts of gray hair hang down over the man's shoulder, and the ends sink into the sea below.

From behind her back the spotty girl shows a skull. "This human remnant, removed from the cave earlier, is about thirty thousand years old. A descendant of this man would still be sharpening his stone ax here in the bush if his contemporaries—homo sapiens half a world away—hadn't come to the idea to split the atom. It was that which brought progress here."

Our men would have speared her for that. I should not look at that skull. No woman has ever been allowed to see Marain Cave or the bones placed there. The spotty girl moves closer and leans on the split boulder for a while, patting the rock. Then she walks a few steps away to face the mountain. She waits silently for the cameraman to replace one of the film rolls and drag the three-legged stand away from the split rock to get a better view of the summit.

The cloud head has drifted closer, heading toward the penin-

177

sula. The hair, no longer trailing in the sea, is caught by a breeze and flutters over the deep, empty field of the sky. I think it is one of our fellows. I cannot say where I have seen him before, but the face looks as though it has been around longer than one can remember. What does Djanbuwal look like? Just like a tribal elder. I suppose.

"From the promenade . . ."

The sudden burst of noise from a jackhammer floods the air. She raises a hand as if to halt the metallic tide, but instead a new noise breaks out and both echo against the cloud. A long jackhammer, outlined by the gray mass, appears on the cloud and begins jerking against the body of a woman. Dust billows from a deep hollow between her legs. The cloud drifts closer, and the rattling sounds louder.

The girl licks her dry lips with her tongue. "From the promenade down at the bay, right up to the summit of the mountain, a wide path will run, paved with strange, flat rocks called *dugaruru*, the reproductive property of each native woman."

While she was talking, the girl held up one of the stones in the air. There is a split across it with a piece about to fall off. Yes, it is the same one that was given to me in town to pound cycad nuts on, the one that disappeared from the cage. The girl slid her fingers across the flat surface and then blew hard on them to drive the dust off.

"The legend says that each woman should have one of these stones inside her in order to conceive. Look, there are piles of them here—millions—gathered from all over the reserves, ready to be set in concrete."

When she is heard on the box again, the girl and the stone will be seen. I wonder who she will be talking to this time—Doctor Cross—wherever he has gone, to the white man's Land of the Dead or ours—she will never reach him again. Perhaps Ranger will have something to say, showing his empty sleeve

178

and telling the others that it was blown off by blasting rocks. He has a good voice and could make it sound mellow and soft. The whites would swallow every word of it. If he lives long enough to see the end of this mountain and the other one . . . no, after Mount Wawalag the land ends . . . if he is going to dig farther he has to ask Jesus or Justice to come along and empty the sea so that he can blast the rocks that rest on the deep bottom.

"The escarpment walls and the mountain summit will be chiseled into a spectacular monument to commemorate the decades of mineral development in the reserve. Actually, it was the uranium prospector who opened up this country to progress. Imagine the endurance and sacrifice the men had to go through while they explored this Stone Age country—a most remote and often hostile part of the world."

The cloud has banked up in the sky like an immense wave ready to break, still looking much like a face but huge and drifting fast. A long strip of the white mass looms over the peninsula and . . . it looks like a hand holding *barlait* ready to strike.

A wandering fly was about to land on the girl's lip, but it was suddenly sucked into her mouth. The insect must have become stuck inside her throat; she struggles with an irritating cough and then pounds her chest with both fists. The cameraman rushes up with a flask of water; the girl gargles and then speaks a few words to see if her voice is all right.

"The two pillars on the summit there, known as the sisters, have to be reshaped thus to symbolize the new cult. On them will rest a huge U-sign which, coated by a luminous substance, would be visible from the far sea. Cynics say that even the tribal spirits from Bralgu will get a glimpse of it." She came closer to the camera.

The ancestor in the sky places his *larban* on the spear-thrower. The *balandas* are still there on the cloud, ripping one

179

of the Wawalags with jackhammers. The cloud hollows, showing the wounds from the white man's tools. The dust billows and then whirls.

"It is a relatively short distance from those pillars down to Marain Cave. So, after decades of being on opposite sides of the nuclear debate, and after bitter arguments, Doctor Cross and the miners are to share the mountain for eternity."

Something has happened to the mountain. The ground trembles for a moment or two and one of the sisters falls. The rock slides over the scarp below the summit and rolls down the slopes with the sound of thunder. The *balandas* flee, leaving the car, their gear and even their water flasks. The huge boulder hurtles by, thumping the ground and making the earth shiver. Then, as it leaps farther out, it sends pieces of peeling crust flying everywhere. A half built house disappears before you can blink your eyes. After it comes rows of fences, the crushed timber thrown high off the ground and left spinning in the air. A part of the pub wall is cut down and a moment later a whole wing of the building caves into a pile of boulders. The mast with the sign loses its balance, begins to fall, and then stops suspended in the air held by some unknown force.

Our mighty ancestor from Bralgu has come!

CHAPTER TWO

Not much of Marain Cave can be seen, only a few wide gaps between the large masses of rocks, each of them leading to the interior of the cave. Perhaps there is more to it when you walk inside, but each entrance is sealed with heavy metal mesh bolted to the rocks, and only those people who are brought by the *balandas* are let in.

The metallic noises from the reshaping of the mountain hang in the air, though they are less noisy here, for the cave looks to the south, toward Upper Valley and *nongaru* billabong. The elders would not like to see a woman around here, but that does not matter any longer. I have not seen a single fellow of ours since I came back to the country. A kick in the depths of my belly—Urban! It's you there, my boy! Hold on, I must lean against the rocks. Climbing up the mountain must have upset you. Calm down, little one. Look, we can see our country from here. The place is not as pretty as it used to be; the rocks are fast turning into dust and the trees . . . no bark left. If those bare trunks are given *dal* ("magic to talk"), the cry will be heard all the way to Bralgu.

181

A long stick looking much like an old spear is hanging down the wall for me to grab and climb up to the top of the scarp. Yes, I thought someone would be there. The shadow of a bearded man falls on the boulder. "Don't slip on the rocks—you'll both be hurt, you and *wadu*."

Marngit is now carrying a hollow spear-thrower and a dilly bag hangs from his neck. From whichever *mala* they come, old men are like each other and speak with the voice of a spirit. Would he chide me for coming here? Though the cave has been disturbed and the *balandas* might have settled here for good, it is our place and sacred to all of us. "No woman goes there except when she dies," *momo* taught me. Only the tribal elders are allowed to come here, because they know how to talk to the spirits.

"I should not be here—the place is sacred." I climbed on top of the scrap.

The beard has lost its bright color. "You had to come."

When they came here the elders would bring their *didjeridu* and *bilma*, for these two speak the lingo known to the dead. When common words are spoken instead of the chanting, a slip of the tongue, or a sound in anger, even though not ill meant, can offend the spirits and bring a curse on the tribe and the country.

"Who have the whites locked up down there?" I glanced at the compound below the scarp.

A gale suddenly sweeps over the boulders, lashing against Marngit's face, though his hair, stiff with dust, hardly stirs: "The black man, who else does the country belong to?"

If the elders had gathered here again for the ceremony there would have been no room to dance. The compound has enclosed the small plateau, and a dwelling has been built inside to house the guard. No elder would like to hold the sacred ceremony under the white man's window.

182

"I'm glad you made that journey." Even Marngit's eyebrows are hardened with dust.

"Can a child be born away from his country?"

"If he does he'll not be part of our sacred world. The country you are born in is your father."

No, I would rather not say anything about Plonk; Marngit would not like to hear about him, not here and . . . he must know all about it already. He might have come to see poor mother in her dreams; yes, it is up to them to talk about it, not me.

I have never been on the scarp before, not even near it. The southern flanks of the mountain look far less steep than the other parts, while at slopes, the ground pauses here and there, forming small plateaus and then sliding smoothly into the plain that stretches toward the mainland and far beyond to the horizon. The country has a grayish face, as though it is coated with early morning dew and . . . no, it could not be dew . . . the bush shows its age like the beard of an old man, forgotten by his own people and the spirits as well; it looks not so much gray as ashen. The leaves and grass have long gone, leaving behind the bare skin of the ground. The boulders that rolled down from the scarp in the time of our ancestors, or even long before, lie scattered around. And though they might be immense, from a distance they look like turtle eggs washed onto the shore.

"They're grinding the stones into dust." The eyes of the old man look sore and wet. "I hear the country crying night and day."

"Yes, I hear it too; it sounds like a dingo caught in a trap." I should ask him what has happened to our people.

"Everything is turning into rocks fast—humans and animals alike. Even the trees have become skeletons."

In the valley far down beyond the fringe of the slopes, there is a dark patch encircled by a green ring. Good, there is still some

183

life; it must be . . . yes, the billabong at *nongaru*, the ceremonial ground. Two rivers flow out of it, but not now; both beds are dry by the look of them. Malgu, which stretches westward, has lost all its trees and the strip of dead gums along the banks looks from here like a trail of ash going all the way to the edge of Mangrove Bay. Gunga, which flowed to the east, looks . . . the river has vanished. Instead of its valley there is a stretch of dug-up ground extending down to the Red Cliff, fringed by the white foam of the rising tide. Across the river, a low cloud of red dust veils the ugly face of the country. The sound of distant thunder floats through the air, but it comes from the ground not the sky; it hovers above the skeletons of the dead trees and bounces back from the rocks of the scarp. The immense monster has crawled out of the sea and begun to tear the earth apart again.

Marngit walks to a large slab of rock and, beckoning me to follow, crawls through the narrow passage. I must step slowly. Hold on, Urban, we have to squeeze through here. It's a short passage; be brave, my boy. The gap'll widen soon.

I follow to the edge of a large opening that stretches deep down between the rocks like a well and ends on the dusty ground of the cave. Not much can be heard and the entrance cannot be seen, but it is not far off. The bars and the metal mesh of the gate cast their shadow on the rocks nearby; the sun had found its way in, but it must have been reflected inside from the outer windows of a building.

"There are ways to make you talk." Yes, I have heard that voice before, not so dry and harsh, though, but the whites know how to stress their words to make you fear them more. "We've invented a gadget to do the job; it can suck the fluid out of your spine."

Moving over the slab a bit farther, I can see Ure down there now. His legs are hoisted up with iron straps, leaving his suspended body to hang down with his back against the rock.

"If you are caught filing that chain again, you'll be hung up by your neck next time."

From above, the man hanging up looks much longer, with his limbs extending into the abyss. Perhaps the body is trying to stretch as far as it can, hoping it will break and so free the strangled soul. Ure's eyes are closed. At least I assume so; they are sunk in deep hollows. Is he alive?

A white hand with a tattooed cross above the wrist reaches for Ure's hair and swings his head up. "Abo martyr!—what a bloody fool."

One of Ure's feet moves; the nail has gone from the big toe, leaving a lump of clotted blood. It must be an old wound; a long red line runs down his leg to the thigh, disappearing into the pubic hair.

Redhead looms over Ure. "Your spookies did not come to fetch you—that would've save us both trouble."

Ure opens his mouth, but instead of words only his dry tongue comes out.

"Would you like any more tucker, I could double the ration to two bowls of fish a day?"

The dry mouth gasps for words. "W-w-w-water."

"The food here is a bit salty, I agree. Sea water is all we have for your folks these days."

Ure's mouth stays open for a while, but no sound comes out.

"Those ancestors of yours had better do something instead of sitting on their arses. It hasn't rained for years."

Ure's head has lifted up for the words to come out. "It will never rain!"

"We aren't going to pray to witch doctors. We have quite a plant down on the beach; it converts salt water into drinkable stuff, enough of it for everyone."

"What about us, the trees and the birds?"

"Bugger 'em, we only want the rocks! Here, have a drink."
He drops Ure's head and empties a water bag over his face.

Can a man drink when he is hanging upside down? Ure must
have caught some of the water in his mouth and is struggling to
swallow it, but even that amount refuses to be drawn up and
runs out. His mouth opens again, mumbling at the wet patch
left on the ground below.

Redhead tosses away the empty bag. "I might get you some
more later on. Let's do our paperwork first, hmm?" Ure is let
down slowly. "That old brother of yours was less of a tough nut
to crack. He actually volunteered to sign the paper for us. It was
all settled amicably."

"What?"

"The deal. Our boss felt generous enough to forget all about
the lost hand and Bungul forgot all about the tribal land. An eye
for an eye, we call it."

"He signed nothing!"

"Not quite. He had a heart attack as soon as he was handed
the pen. Too much excitement for the simple soul, the boss
thinks. See how you make out . . ."

Ure swings his head away from the paper.

"Don't shy off—just make a cross. We were going to give
Bungul a pension—a fish and a coconut every day. He told us it
was you that speared the boss. A white man's hand is worth
more than a whole tribe of you blacks, so let's square, hmm?"

"You've taken the land already!"

"The boss wants an honest deal." The white man lights a
cigarette. "Have a smoke . . . try it. Look, you don't need the
land any longer . . . there won't be any more black kids born.
The old doc has seen to it. We strangled the snake that laid the
eggs. There'll only be a few half-caste brats here and there, but
they don't have any rights to land. It's your tribal law, not ours,
that says that."

Ure grabs a handful of damp soil from the ground and holds it against his mouth.

"The document is already drafted. 'I, Ure of Narku, in a sober state of mind, give all my land on the Djungau Peninsula to be cared for by the Adder Corporation.' That means, my friend, that the whites are going to water every single tree in the bush. Here, make a cross like this . . . to say that the paper has been read to you."

"The trees . . . they have all died already."

"Don't worry, old fella, every single leaf will be brought back to life again: grass, animals, birds—the lot. We have the technology and know-how to do it. We have even been on the moon; it will be green too."

Ure grabs another handful of soil. Redhead takes a small transistorlike box out of his pocket. "Hallo, my old friend; come to your senses. Your world and mine will be grateful to us for this endeavor. The corporation . . ." It is Ranger, sounding not as when I heard him last but as he sounded when seen on the TV screen. Something must have gone wrong; his voice has suddenly been cut off and Redhead strikes at the transistor a few times. "We have appointed you the governor of the reserve, the first black man ever to be so honored. A cosy residence has been built for you at Durana Island; the island will be yours. When you feel like hopping over for a visit to Bralgu just ask for my helicopter—at your service any time." Redhead held out a sheet of paper: "Sign here!"

The handful of wet earth splatters onto the paper. Redhead hurriedly hoists Ure up again. "I'll get someone else to do it. By our law, all men are equal, regardless of color."

The mountain suddenly trembles again. I could feel the rocks shaking for a moment or two, and it looked as if the wall of cliffs was about to slide down over the slopes below. From the compound, I heard a whistle and the whining of a siren. No, I

187

had better not run down the mountain slopes; there are no bushes or leaves around to shelter me. It is much safer to hold on to the cliff and let the rocks shield me until dusk, then head straight to . . . where is there to go? The only green patch around here is the billabong down at Upper Valley. There should be some of our people there; they flock to water like the animals and birds.

A rattling sound floats through the air and bounces against the wall of the scarp—a helicopter! I cannot see the machine yet; it will take a while to appear above the skeletons of the trees. I had better look for a shelter beneath the rock, the way the reptiles do. I should be careful of my grown belly. Urban would not like me to crawl under. Yes, my dear boy, we will lie beside the boulder—the color of our skin hardly differs from that of the rock.

The palm fronds are dark green and the grass is spear high. It looks as though it has been raining for a whole long season. Even the flowers are back—a tall, old *banksia* droops under a heavy load of cones as the new life springs out from the tough, stunted trunks. Muru sniffs the bushes and then, as his snout rises to probe the air, his ears prick up searching for the sound. There is no one about, furry. Our friends are far away, and the *balandas* . . . there're no young girls here to attract them.

Across the billabong, far away toward the mainland, the column of a willy-willy burrows into the sky. It will be dry and dusty farther into the bush. The trees have long since turned into ghostly skeletons, and the scrub was wiped out long ago. What a pity this patch of green does not go farther, for if the drought grips the land for much longer, the plants will forget what leaves look like.

The dog still sniffs the air and lifts his leg on the bushes. Calm down, Muru! Maybe he is wary of being here. Are dogs allowed on sacred ground?

188

Someone must have been on *nongaru* ground to care for the trees. Even small stretches of Malgu River, a short distance downstream from the billabong, are wrapped in green. Perhaps the spirits have been taking care of the bush and making it grow again. They have their own way of sneaking water in from Bralgu, or perhaps they let a shower come during the night when the *balandas* could not see it. A finger count of seasons must have passed since the last ceremony was held here; there is no *dagu*. A storm or a willy-willy might have torn through here, blowing off every branch. The women's shades are never made to last, and the withered leaves fall off the branches as soon as the ceremony is over. Hold on, one is still there; it looks big enough to shelter a whole group of girls. No, it is only an uprooted tree, not *dagu*. I wonder . . . perhaps the spirits knocked down the tree when they brought the water to the billabong. How did they get so much water? The pool is too big for them to have carried it in bark buckets. Maybe they sang *dal* and let magic make the water spring out of the ground; it could not have come from the sky. *Nara* ("foliage") is coated with a heavy layer of dust. In the sunlight it appears reddish, and the leaves look like the dying glow of coals half sunk in ashes.

Muru sits at the edge of the billabong. Why is the dog staring at the water? It should be about time for Jogu, my sister, to be brought here, become *bala* and . . . no, she would have gone through the initiation years ago. I doubt if she was betrothed when I was here. However, she should be married by now, probably living with her *duwei* down near Mangrove Bay. We Galwan girls cannot marry Jiridja men; each of us had to go to a neighboring clan.

Muru is still staring at the billabong, his snout pointing at the water. A flying fox might have gone that way, leaving a scent trail behind. There is no sound; the animal must have flitted by silently.

Look what has happened to *murlg*. Only two forked sticks are

189

left; one has been crushed into a mass of splinters and pounded into the ground by some immense weight. The bulldozers must have gone right through, making caterpillar marks. The *balandas* have dug out a large trench; it looks as if it stretches across the country all the way to the Mount Wawalag slopes and the place where they built the new settlements and . . . here they went straight through *nongaru*, ripped out all the guts from the ground and then buried them again. Perhaps they sneaked a long pipe through the ground and let it soak up the water from the billabong and then carried it to the *balandas*, inside the white men's homes. The spirits will be angry when they find this out. The whites use so much water. They say their skin is lighter because it is washed so often. Our ancestors in Bralgu had better do something about it before this place dries up, too.

Look, Marngit is here. He has gathered the scattered saplings from the old hut and there, at the far end of *nongaru*, propped them up to make a tent shape for a new shelter. Some leafy branches have been brought in too, and together with fronds they will make a cover, not so much to keep out the rain as the sun and the dust.

"It is good that you have come; *murlg*, my home, is just about ready."

"What a nice shelter!" It looks small inside, only room for me and the child when it comes; perhaps there is no need for it to be bigger.

"It is near the billabong, just as the Wawalags had theirs."

"How long does it take for a tribe to grow?"

The medicine man wiped his eyes. "The people have not gone for good; they have been changed into insects, fish or stars. They are waiting to come back again."

"How soon?"

"The *balandas* are not here forever. They have their own world to fall back on. As soon as they have enough rocks they

190

will leave."

It should be all right. The people—both Galwan and Narku tribes—will come to life just as new shoots come up from seeds after a long drought or a bushfire has swept through. The country is *walg* of a huge mother, and it brings to life not only humans but everything from a tiny patch of moss to a whole forest. However, for anything to grow—fish, trees or man—you need good rain, and the clouds will always come if our fellows are here to call them. I hope Wanba still flies around in the bushes and has not been driven off; without the pigeon to sound the call at first light, the fellows will never gather on the ground to build a women's shade and prepare *nongaru* for the big ceremony to lure the clouds into rolling over the mainland.

"Can I go inside?"

"It is yours, as warm and soft as a nest." The man spreads an armful of softened bark over the ground and then dashes out into the bush to get some more.

There should be some tucker about, yams are not hard to come by near water. You should not gather food at *nongaru* or step into the billabong, but the spirits . . . they were all humans once and know what it is like to have a belly rumbling day and night. If there is food around I could hang on here and wait for the people to come back. Look, there are whole groves of cabbage palms with their fronds looming above the dark green face of the water. It looks just like Muruwul water hole as it was painted on the sheet of bark. Maybe I must go through it like the Wawalags and give birth to a child so that the spirits will see to it that life starts up again, rolling out like a long line stretching from a ball of string. Will I have to be swallowed by Julungul as the sisters were—the child and the dog too? Perhaps we will all slide down into the serpent's belly. But what does it matter, the spirits know what is best for us. I will stay inside the python asleep and wake up only when I am vomited out. Julungul will

191

lick us all clean and leave us to begin a new life.

The old man comes back from the bush bringing no paper-bark, but on his arm perches a bird—Wanba! The pigeon looks tiny, with wet feathers pressed flat to its body. The bird seems to have shrunk to the size of a chick; its eyes are half closed, its head sways and then droops. One of the pigeon's wings hangs down, the pinions touching the elder's arm and . . . yes, it must have an upset belly; the feathers at the back are covered with the mess.

"It was stuck in the murk at the edge of the water." The old man lifts his arm but instead of taking off, the bird clings to him and makes no move to spread its wings.

"Should Wanba rest for a while?"

"It stinks around here, even the flies will have their guts ripped out."

"Where can we go?"

The man said nothing; his arms cradled the bird against his chest.

"What about Mangrove Bay?" I whisper.

"It's your *duwei*'s country and the child's *babaru*. Yes, you should go to the place."

"Any life left there?"

"Only scraps chucked away by the *balandas*."

"Could we live on it?"

"It might just see you through."

The rattling of a helicopter is suddenly heard, and a moment later the machine spins out from the edge of the forest. I had better dash behind the bushes and hide under the palm fronds. Around the water the ground feels soft and I have to watch so as not to get bogged. Phew, it stinks! I do not think Julungul would like to live in that murk. Something is floating on the surface of the billabong; no, it is not lily pads. There are dark patches scattered here and there. The billabong looks like a face, with a

192

good part of it covered with a crust. Near the edge of the pool, some of the floating mass has drifted close to a cabbage palm; the swaying fronds tickle the water, and the floating crust is pushed back. One of the fronds has a piece of tissue paper stuck to it. No, it is more like cotton wool. Some white woman must have chucked it out when her bleeding time had passed. The air here . . . it smells like a *dugong* that has been washed ashore and left rotting for some days.

A woman comes out of a pandanus grove and walks through the shallow part of the billabong. Maybe . . . would it be Jogu? I cannot see her face properly; her body is bent. She only straightens up now and then when her hands pull *ragia* out of the mud to place it in the bag hanging from her neck. Her hair has fallen over her face. She straightens up and brushes it back with a sweep of her arm. She has just pulled out a good chunk of root, which she splashes in the water to wash off the mud; then she bites a piece out of it before chucking the tucker in her bag. When she comes to shore I will tell her that the water is bad. The whites have pumped out all their mess from the settlement, and the stuff stinks. It will kill humans and spirits alike. The dog hardly stops lifting his leg to mark every bush on the bank. She is off. Rising into the air, she flutters for a while, then glides over the clumps of bamboos and disappears from *nongaru*.

A huge shadow moves over *nongaru* and stops. The metal beast comes down on the ground; the door of the machine swings open and Wurulu looks out. In her hand she has something . . . some sort of funnel; she holds it against her mouth and calls, "Julie . . . come here. They brought some food . . . Julie . . ."

Why is her voice quivering?

"Julie . . . Julie, come out."

I dreamed once that Wurulu was feeding my dog Muru from her hand: "We'd better not teach you to eat with fork, when you

193

break free you could starve in the bush without cutlery." That must have happened while I was in the enclosure—a whole world behind now.

"Julie . . . take care . . ."

She is breaking down. The voice rises. "Stay away. Take no food. Julie, run bush . . . Jul . . ."

A hand from inside the helicopter grabs the amplifier from her. The machine takes off hastily and then it hovers in the air above the trees. Luckily there is thick *nara* ("foliage"); even an eagle could miss its prey hiding under the fronds. I wonder whether they can see Malabin. She does not seem to have taken any notice of the machine; she holds a lily bulb as big as a fist and moves her hand over it to admire its size, then a smile dawns on her face. A cloud of dust, blown off the leaves by the hovering machine, spreads over the water and drowns her. For a moment or two only a pair of eyes are to be seen, red and weeping. Then they too sink into the cloud.

"Julie, come out. We have brought you some food. Julie . . ." It is a man's voice now.

From the helicopter, a cage is sent down. It comes close to the ground, almost to within a hand's reach, and sways about as the machine flies over the billabong. The man's voice calls again, but his words float across the water to the pandanus grove and bounce back, weakened and half drowned by the rattle of the machine. The helicopter hovers above the tops of the trees for a while. Then, tired of hanging around, it heads back toward Mount Wawalag and disappears beyond the edge of the forest.

194

CHAPTER
THREE

A sudden wriggle, then a kick, comes from my *walg*. Hold on,
Urban, the walking must be hard on you, too. It is the wrong
time of day to be wandering about. Even the scorpions have dug
in for shelter.

It is more than a one-camp journey to Mangrove Bay. The
sun is heading for the top of the sky, and I had better look around
for some deep shade and not sweat much, for water is hard to
find. Perhaps I should move only during the night; the bare
ground is much cooler then, and a breeze comes from the sea. It
would be hard to wander off in the bush now. The whites have
cleared a wide track that begins in the cloud of dust that always
sits on the upper part of the Gunga River now, rumbling day
and night like a wounded beast.

The track, much wider than any road I have ever seen, cuts
through the bush as straight as the flight of a spear, pausing on a
small rise at the foot of the mountain, and then heads along the
peninsula toward the end of the land. Through the middle of it
stretches a low structure of metal girders, and on top of them, a
belt carrying rocks slides over an endless chain of rollers. I had

195

better keep on walking to the rise. It is hardly a voice away, and there is a corrugated iron tower on top, with a wide opening for the belt and rocks to go through.

Little Urban is getting moody again. How he can kick! Walking on this rough ground, all covered with loose soil and rocks, is very tricky. Dust has gathered in the deeper holes and I only find them when my foot plunges in. I must stop for a while and sit on that stump. No, it is the remains of a dead anthill the bulldozer has cleared almost to the ground. Steady, steady, little boy! That hurts, that sharp kick! I did not make the country so rough! Look, did I ever tell you about the bees? I know a hollow tree they nest in, packed with *jarban* ("honey").

The rise is not far off now. If there are no cars at that tower the whites will not be there; in bush like this the *balandas* never travel without their machines. I should sneak in quickly. There must be a water bag or tap somewhere; there is sure to be one in the dunny. It might be much safer to wait until nightfall, but the end of the day is a long way away and by then, my throat will be stone dry. I had better have a drink now and look for some shade.

No one has been here today; the footprints in the dust are old and faint. The *balandas* must come here only occasionally to pat their machine and say a nice word or two to it before driving off and leaving the metal beast to rumble on, slaving for them. I wonder . . . yes, there is a tap right beside the wall of that small shed. If the whites are right, this is sea water, but I doubt it; the taste is no different. Maybe it comes from a deep bore or perhaps the boats bring it in when they come: there is a convoy of them down in the bay. They look like a flock of seagulls, and whenever I face toward the open sea I can always see one or two passing the strait of Balanda Cape. These boats do not show a line of smoke like the one *momo* told me about. Perhaps they have not come for humans, but they are after something,

196

otherwise they would never sail up the bay.

A car has suddenly pulled up in front of the building. It is too late to dash out now. Hold on, Urban, don't kick. We have to be silent and calm. It could be a trap . . . let's stay inside and hope that luck will be on our side. It stinks in here, and the whites will not come in unless they have an urge to unload themselves. There is a small window, high up, but if I climb up on the toilet I can get a good view through the broken louvres. Hold on, my boy. Luckily no one is chasing us. It is that girl again, with her mob and their cameras; this time they even have Plonk with them. What are they going to do with the fool, I wonder. He wears tough, heavy boots and the canvas hat. He looks clumsy in that white man's gear, and the girl has to help him climb up to the driver's seat of a large bulldozer parked near the window. I hope he is not going to drive. The machine is made to tear the country apart and level the hills; it would take only a moment to flatten the whole building. The girl waits for the camera to be set on its legs and then begins to speak into the microphone: "When Adder arrived here, the aborigines were in a hurry to leave for Bralgu, especially their chief, Bungul. He had no time to put his signature to the paper that would hand the tribal land over to its new custodians."

A stubborn fly hovers around the girl's face; she closes her mouth and waits until the insect buzzes off.

"Chief Bungul was a close relative of Marngit, that informant of the late Doctor Cross; so is Johnny Walker, a man of the new generation. According to tribal custom, when a man is born outside tribal territory, he has no ritual rights and no land rights either."

Something is troubling Plonk, the whining sound of the camera or the girl's voice? He taps his head, waits for a moment then slams his fist against his helmet several times.

The girl licks her dry lips. "In respect of traditional tribal law,

197

Adder holds the land in trust until the rightful owner is found. The corporation has appointed Johnny Walker as the executor of the tribal estate. How are the whites treating you, Johnny?"

Why do they have to change his name. Plonk is *balandas'* word, not ours.

Plonk left the lever he was holding, and his hand moved as if to knock his head, but remembering suddenly that the microphone rod looming above him was expecting words, he struggles with his mouth.

"G . . . g . . . g. . . ." His mouth has been straightened.

" 'Good' . . . thank you . . . and what about the mining royalty coming to the trust?"

"E . . . e . . . . e . . ."

" 'Excellent, it looks excellent.' If Marngit and your other ancestors were here, would they be pleased with this arrangement, too?"

"N . . . n . . . n . . ."

" 'Naturally'; I see. Johnny, would they also be happy with the white man being here?"

"O . . . o . . . o . . ."

" 'Of course' . . . yes. Tell me, do you still worship your ancestors—hold on to your traditional beliefs?"

"C . . . c . . . c . . ."

" 'Christian,' you are Christian now! How has this sudden change in outlook affected you?"

"I . . . I . . . I . . ."

" 'Ideally'; I see. Now tell me, how do you feel about the great progress that Adder has brought? Say it in your tribal lingo, please."

"D . . . d . . . *dagu win!*"

"That means 'dinkum'—'wonderful.' " The girl steps back from the machine and looks into the camera. "As you see, Johnny Walker has not mastered English yet and is also slightly

198

handicapped. He has recently undergone plastic surgery. Hopefully his speech defect will improve."

Plonk wants to say something else, perhaps what *dagu* really means. He knocks his fist against his helmet several times, but when he remains unnoticed he becomes angry and slams his hand against the panel of the scraper instead and mumbles the beginning of a word: "E . . . e . . . . e . . ."

The girl is still turned toward the camera. "He has actually made a remarkable start, and for a while he was the protégé of the late Doctor Cross. But the sudden adaptation to the new culture affected his ability to talk. Johnny Walker is of exceptional IQ and chief contributor to the sperm bank. He and others will be the incognito fathers of the next generation of aborigines."

This, or something else, upset Plonk, because he jumps down onto the ground and turns to face one of the front tires of the scraper while at the same time struggling to open his fly. Redhead calls out to him and points to the toilet block. I had better lock the door in case he comes this way. But even if he sees me it would be quite a strain for him to explain, and the whites would not believe a word of it.

Now the girl has moved closer to the belt and watches it carrying the load of rocks down the gentle slopes, across the swamp at the edge of Mangrove Bay and down to Balanda Cape. She waits, then lifts one of the red stones from the belt and looks at it. "Uranium! Day and night, these rocks travel by conveyor belt from the field about thirty kilometers inland, past the station here, and end up to the enrichment plant on the bay."

Not far from the rise, a part of the Wawalag slopes has been sliced off, leaving a bare wall. The mountain, trimmed on this side, looks as though it has retreated from the sea and is stretching up toward the sky to make it harder for the *balandas* to climb up and reach the rocks.

199

"Every minute this belt operates, down passes enough precious rock to light Paris, London, Tokyo and New York. The equivalent of that energy could fly a manned spacecraft to the moon and back many times. The power of your dishwasher, home computer, electric tin opener, juice extractor, sauna, film projector and electric toothbrush shall all come from here. While I have been chatting to you, enough uranium to melt the entire winter snow of Europe has passed along this belt."

The conveyor belt has cut across the mangroves, filling in half the swamp. The bare earth has been pounded hard, and not even a patch of moss will grow there now. Several large boulders lie on the barren field like forgotten crops; it must have been hard for even the whites to shift them, and the ground near them looks as if a willy-willy has galloped across the plain, leaving behind an immense cloud of dust that spirals up to the sky, hiding a whole chunk of the peninsula.

"Those hills at the conveyor belt terminus are the stock pile; each one contains enough uranium ore to split the earth."

On the rest of the swamp, the trees are dead, the dry wood of the branches a pale color against the dark red background. Is the color in the mud or the water, I wonder? Whatever evil has struck the swamp, the crabs will not like it, and they too will have to go soon. Once the roots of the mangrove trees rot, it is an end to their safe home. Small patches of cleared forest are showing; some of the trees must have gone. It will not be long before the rest of them slide down into the mud. The swamp will look like a heap of bones, but not for long. Once the trees rot, that whole part of the country will be bare marsh—not even a fly will come near it for fear of becoming bogged.

"Those tall towers behind the stockpile are part of the enrichment plant. The enriched uranium that those monsters would produce in years to come will be equivalent to the power of the oil reserves of the whole Arab world. 'Sheikhs, eat your

200

hearts out,' is a saying here."

Farther up the bay, toward the mouth of the Malgu River, the sun bounces off the muddy shore, glistening on a trail of mounds that lay scattered along the edge of the water. They must be *dugongs* washed ashore; no other fish could be seen from such a distance. A flock of seagulls circles above the carcasses, sending out calls that ricochet from the edge of the forest and fly across the bay to the mainland.

"The presence of the plant has affected the color of the sea. There is no evidence, however, that is has done any harm to the life in the water. Authorities have so far received no complaints, either from humans or fish."

The water in the bay has become red. From here it looks like a large patch of blood spilled on the dusty ground. When this life finishes and another comes, I would not like to be reborn as a crab; I always thought that they were the happiest lot, living on land or water and enjoying the best of both worlds, but it looks as though the country around here will never be a fit place to live in.

Gently, gently, my boy—ouch! I'll sit down—is that better now? The country out there looks like a skinned carcass. It makes you feel . . . it gets you in the guts, doesn't it? My boy, the world looks too dusty and ugly for you to come into. Let's hope that Djanbuwal, our ancestor, will be here soon to sort everything out. You'll hear him coming, my boy.

CHAPTER FOUR

Man does not grow differently from birds or reptiles. Just as turtles return to the sandy beach each year to lay a clutch of eggs and brolgas come to the salty claypan to roost, humans come back too—to *murlg*. My home, here I come.

There is not much of it left, the trunk of a large paperbark has come down, this season or the one before, and flattened half of it. Only two of *darbal* ("forked posts") remain standing; the other two have collapsed, pulling down most of the saplings from the platform for resting on during the Wet. The bark roof above the platform has been blown off in a gale; they often come up from Balanda Cape and race across the swampy plain. Yinguamba and Djulgu could not keep the hut standing against the wind. A pair of young hands are needed if there is no man around to keep the place safe.

I will have to try to lift the fallen poles. They will be heavy, but dry timber is not hard to handle. When I have dragged the stilts from under the fallen tree, the old post holes will have to be cleared out so that the *darbal* will slide in again. With the four poles all up, the roof may still be far off, but the shape of the hut can be seen. It should not take long to build it again. How long is it since Bungul . . . no, since my *duwei* left; he was taken away, surely. No black man could have sat still and watched the bulldozers carving up the hills and tearing into the land. And when you are an elder you have to fight, not only for your *babaru* but to stand up for the whole tribe.

The hole in the ground has to be cleared of the rotting stump and fallen earth before the post is put in again. Yinguamba and Djulgu might come soon to give me a hand with the timber. They must have been told that I am back. Marngit, at least, must have visited their dreams to tell them all about it.

A stone ax with its handle long gone lies on the ground, partly sunk into the dust; the tool must have been used when the hut was built. Marngit must have brought it to his brother and told him, probably, that the whites had decided to make hatchets instead of guns and that Doctor Cross wanted every black man to have new tools. My *duwei* might not have believed every word he was told, but the ax cuts well, nevertheless. Look, its blade still feels sharp. I had better not press my thumb against it too hard. Even without a handle it can still be used for knocking stumps off branches for making into the platform if nothing else. The platform above the fork of the posts must be high up. The country is dead dry now, but the clouds might come any day now if the spirits make up their minds to send Djanbuwal to flash his spear across the sky. When he comes, the thunder and roar of the storm will make the white man and his machine shiver like a tail dropped by a lizard. I hope the roof will be up by then. Yes, Urban, you wouldn't like us to be bogged in the swamp.

There is no sign of those two yet; they should come soon. When they are wandering through the bush, women are always on the lookout for yams or reptiles to catch for their dinner. They might have chased a goanna up a tree; you have to wait

203

half a day before it climbs down again. I could make a fire and have plenty of hot coals ready in case it is a big catch. No, I should forget all about that; smoke gives you away too easily. The *balandas* do not seem to be around so much, but the plant down there never stops rattling and hissing, hardly a voice away.

It does not matter how heavy the storm is when it comes or how long it lasts once the Wet sweeps the country; *murlg* stands up to it if it is properly built. The country slopes down to Balanda Cape from Mount Wawalag, then sinks into the swamp, leaving hardly any ground showing, only the tops of the trees scattered here and there. The water could come a good way up the post as well, but it would never reach the platform. When the child comes . . . what a sharp kick! A few more like that will rip my belly open. C'mon, my boy, calm down. Don't lose your temper with me. The child should come soon—no more than a few days, I reckon. Let's look at our home, Urban. We couldn't live without a roof when the Wet comes. You have not been here before. When it rains, big swamps swallow up this part of the country, I tell you.

The posts sway; they look like loose teeth; I should search for a handful of pebbles and small rocks to stuff around each one and pound them in to make the structure firm, for if there is water lying around and the ground softens up, the wind could easily blow the hut over. Me, I could swim or hold on to a log and drift with it toward the nearest piece of land, but the *wadu*—the little one—will be too young.

A boulder lies half buried in the ground a spear's throw or two from the hut, its sharp edge looking as if it has been blasted off the mountain. Some *dal*, or more likely the white man and his machines, tossed it in the air and made it land down here. Luckily it did not hit anyone or there would not even be a small piece of uncrushed bone left behind to tell human from animal remains. The rock must have come down on the campfire; bits of charcoal are scattered around, leaving only a dark patch on the disturbed red soil. Yinguamba and Djulgu would not have liked to see their place wiped out. The fellows would feel less pain. They have plenty of other things to care about—hunting in the bush or holding a ceremony—but the woman is the one who worries about the fire, and if you took that away or quenched the flame forever, think first of all the moaning and cursing that would be heard all the way to Bralgu.

No need to worry about steps or look for a notched branch to lean against one of the posts and climb up. The platform can easily be reached by climbing onto the boulder and then up the trunk of the fallen paperbark tree. I could even take the fire up with me and let the flickering light shine again on the trunks of the nearby trees. Yes, women like to take the fire inside *murlg;* the platform has to be covered with rocks and then a layer of mud to keep the hot coals away from the floor.

I wish those two were here to tell me if what I am doing is right. How long will the three of us have to struggle on our own? I thought that when the whites put our man in the lockup, for whatever they were trying to squeeze out of him, they would let him out in the end. Not that the *balandas* like to see any of us go free but because they would grow tired of feeding the poor soul. They are not going to do that to Ure, though. The night before last I dreamed about him. The whites have tripled his chains to make sure that he does not reach either the country here or Bralgu. At least he has been taken away from that cave. Outside, when you can see the sky and the willy-willy crossing the country, it lets you breathe easier.

The roof—should it be made from bark sheets with a layer of mud on top? I think they get the soil from an anthill. First crush it into dust to make mud, and when that is spread over sheets of bark and allowed to dry, it goes so hard that not even the heaviest storm could wash it off the roof. Aah! How he kicks! I can feel it

205

with my hand on my belly.

I hope that Yinguamba and Djulgu will be back; each of them knows about giving birth, and they will help a lot. Maybe they are up in the mountains, hiding among the bluffs so that they can see Durana Island, even by moonlight, and feel closer to Ure. They might light a fire at night so he can see from across the water where to go if he makes it to the mainland. I should go there too. Not now—after Urban comes. Perhaps . . . yes, the women might come here to lead me to their hideout in the hills. When we are together I can go out looking for food while they stay in camp with the boy and keep an eye on the sea in case Ure heads this way. Perhaps I should have made a fire on the ground behind that boulder. The column of smoke will tell them I am back home. Yinguamba will come to fetch me while Djulgu stays in camp to watch for Ure. Yes, the fire tells you where to go. "Never let it go out," *momo* told me. The huts here at the swamp always had a raft. During the Wet the man moves around on it to gather food; the woman left behind has to keep the fire alight so the smoke will show him where to come back to.

Part of the swamp stretches away behind the hut. It is strangely bare and ugly. The water has gone and the mud has become so hard that it looks like a slate shattered in pieces. The Dry has set in for an endless run; the rain that should have come last season and for many seasons before that never turned up, and the face of the earth has creased into an immense web. Instead of rain, the red dust comes, falling over the ground like morning dew; but it does not disappear with the early sun and stays on the ground for good, painting the whole countryside red.

A vast, salty claypan lies between the sea and the swamp, keeping the two apart. A flock of *gururgu* ("brolgas") used to gather there at sunset. They do not perch on trees like other birds but seek the safety of the salty ground. The place will be no

206

good for then now, covered with . . . no, it is not dust but muddy, red stuff; it stinks like rotten eggs. It looks as though the belly of the country has been ripped open and the mess from the torn gut poured in to fill up the claypan.

Whatever has happened above, the ground may still hide a crop underneath; I should make *ganinjari* ("digging stick") and plunge it into the soil; beneath the hard crust of the swamp there are always lily bulbs. You cannot see them, but somehow you know the right spot to strike, just as *gururgu* do when they plunge their long beaks into the ground to pull out roots, seldom missing them. The women are taught by the birds to gather their food that way, too. *Momo* said that the first brolga was a girl once, and had to be taken to *nongaru* for initiation. It happened soon after *warngi* ("sea monster") plundered the country, leaving not even one tree to cut a boomerang from. The man had pierced her *dagu* with his fingers instead. It did her no good, for she turned into a brolga and ran into the bush.

A tuft of hair is hanging on a branch, fluttering in the breeze. Yinguamba must have been here searching for food. She might have hoped for some brolga's eggs, though there are no claw marks on the ground and not a single feather to be seen. The birds have left forever. Farther off, beyond the vast pond of red mud, rises a forest of steel; the towers stretch up toward the sky like giant spears. They rumble, hiss and occasionally puff out a sulfur cloud. It is hard to tell whether it is smoke or steam except that it smells of rotten turtle eggs. Maybe . . . yes, that cloud must have driven Yinguamba and Djulgu away from here. Women do not like hissing noises; you cannot help thinking of a monstrous serpent crawling out of the sea. Hey, steady on, little boy. I'll sit down and keep still for a moment. Is that better now? I'll show you that hollow tree full of honey when you are born. Yinguamba will come with us too; she knows where the bees nest.

I doubt if Ure will be back on the mainland, not for a while.

The whites have him chained up on Durana Island. I watched him the night before last trying to break out and swim away. That white man is still with him, to see that he does not file through his chains. "Here, the whole island's yours since you like the bloody land so much! Drag it away, if you can!" The *balanda* laughs.

A narrow arm of the claypan has extended deep into the surrounding ground, wedging a mass of red mud between the dry crust of the swamp. Muru does not like that smell; he sniffs around, claws the ground and whines. The dog can tell, too, that the smelly stuff has spread from those metal towers and whatever the whites are up to there, those sulfur clouds and the red mud make you want to retch.

The place is no good; no matter how hard I push *ganinjari* into the ground or how often, I cannot find any lily bulbs, not a single one. The crops, like everything else—birds, insects and humans—have gone. Maybe . . . yes, there is a rubbish dump farther away on the edge of the dry swamp; there could be some food there. There is always a pile of old things that the *balandas* have chucked out. I had better sneak in for a look; night would be a better time, but I cannot see a soul around. Perhaps I could find a panel or two of corrugated iron to put on the roof of the hut; a sheet of plastic would be a help, too.

The whites do not look for bush tucker; they carry their own food and even ferry the stuff they drink across the sea. The barges, much larger than those that used to call at Red Cliff before, can always be seen on the way in and out of the bay, passing Balanda Cape. But nothing floats forever, and the *balandas* will grow tired of bringing in tucker and booze and taking away the rocks. Not even *djabari* ("scorpion") will make his home in bare, dry country like this.

Several more tufts of hair lie scattered about. Hold on, Muru. Stand away from the mud. Is that Yinguamba or Djulgu? I cannot tell from the bones. The skull is still partly covered with skin. She must have got bogged or been thrown in by some evil. Her head is poking out of the red mud and one hand too—holding *ganinjari*.

A willy-willy dust column rises into the air. Near the ground the spinning tail of dust is tiny, but higher up the column widens and looks like the shoulders of a man with a hand lifted to throw *larban* ("spear"). The wind gallops across the rubbish dump, tossing the empty plastic containers and the bundles of paper high into the sky. A discarded mattress whirls in the air and lands in the crown of a dead tree. It stays there for a while and then, struggling to free itself, tears down a large branch; suddenly it bursts, and the stuffing clouds the air. The wind cuts across part of the swamp and, heading down toward the stockpile of rocks, wraps the steel towers in a cloud of dust. A roof is tossed up toward the sky. Near the jetty, a sheet of flame flashes out and a moment later a whole building slides down into a funnel of dust. The metal towers sway. One of them falls, puffing out a ball of violet flames; the others are engulfed in sulfur smoke and are sinking from view fast.

Djanbuwal! The ancestor rides through the country on a dry storm, lashing the *balandas*. The whites might put up with it for a while, but not forever. Men grow sick of being hated by the land and the spirits and will leave in the same way that the *balandas* did when they were here before. The peninsula was given to Galwan and Narku by our ancestors and stocked with plants and animals for each *babaru* to live on. At first the ancestors were in no hurry. Let the white man eat as much of the rock as his belly can stand; let the dust lash his pale face and the sun burn his light skin. The harder it is for him, the longer it will be remembered; even his unborn children will have nothing but a curse for him.

209

CHAPTER FIVE

A sharp kick again and I feel my belly being ripped apart. Hold on there, little man, that hurts.

Should I go down from the hut platform? On the ground you can grab a boulder or hold on to one of the bushes around. That might not bring Urban out quicker; it helps to have something to grip instead of your own face and hair. I have put a piece of paperbark in my mouth to hold my teeth apart.

Thunder shatters the sky and travels fast through the dark toward the tribal countries across Mangrove Bay. Stay on the platform. It might not rain, but the dust and sand from the bare ground will fly about, and what is the good of being born if you are choked to death before you can open your eyes to see the world you are coming to.

The cockatoo roosts on a dry tree next to the hut, so close I can see the white feathers in the dark. See, Urban, we're not on our own. In the country here you'll never be alone. The bird moves restlessly, rustles her pinions and goes out of sight. She'll still be here but is searching for a more sheltered spot to perch on. The cockatoo should come inside; there is room for the whole *babaru* (family) here.

The lightning tears the sky again and following the thunder the country falls back into sacred silence. No, it is not so quiet down at the shore: a large ball of blazing light has pushed the dark away from the plant. The whites and all those metal beasts must be scared at night and make the dark retreat like the sea does at low tide. Steady boy, the *balandas* are far from us. Your totem will be the emu; you know, that bird runs faster than the wind. I once saw an emu chased by a helicopter. It almost got away. I'll tell you more about it when . . . aah! You are ripping your poor mother . . .

Muru howls. The cockatoo screeches. It is on the tree still but is hidden by the dark. The bird should be silent at night; perhaps she is trying to tell me something—her fear of the storm? It does not rain, only dry gusts howling in the dark. Grains of sand lash against the hut and part of the roof flies off, opening a view of the dark sky.

Don't be frightened, Urban; it is our ancestor Djanbuwal coming to see you. A new Galwan tribe will grow from you. You know about Wawalag. She had a child and all tribes spread from him later. That wad of bark between my teeth has broken; I have to look for a tougher piece. I could have brought a cloth; there are heaps of old garments and torn blankets on the rubbish dump there, though none of our women ever used that stuff, my mother neither. She was given cotton wad to hold between her teeth while Wurulu fiddled with the injection, and she choked. She came to tell me all about it in my dream. The lightning splits the sky and shows the cockatoo for a moment. The bird perches on a branch above the hut, holding her head sideways with one of the eyes looking down at me.

Steady boy! You have to be wary of whites when you grow up. That emu that was chased by the helicopter, they caught the poor bird with a bait—a piece of bread soaked in whiskey.

211

A vague noise comes from the dark. It is not the cockatoo clapping her beak but something else—not the wind or the sound of an animal but the noise of two oval stones clapping against each other. Aah, don't get so wild, young Urban. Let your mother catch her breath. The hut sways with the force of the wind; Muru must feel that, too, and whimpers from the ground to tell me. I hope the platform will not slide down. Too late to move out now, but as soon as this is all over I'd better go down. The ground will be much safer, and we could sit by the fire sheltering behind the boulder.

Hold on there, little man. Hurt. Your head is out, Urban. The shoulders will soon come, too. I have to touch you gently; your skin is soft. You know that hollow tree packed with honey, it is not in the bush any longer. Only an uprooted stump; I saw it at the rubbish dump . . . aah! You'll see that tree in your dreams, when you grow up and . . . and taste the honey as well.

The platform has brown slippery blood, not sweat. A pity there is no swamp near the hut to wash off the dripping blood. That stuff will smell tomorrow. If it is carried by the wind it could lure scavenging birds and evil spirits. Down at the plant, the *balandas* might smell the blood, too. No white man is seen, however; something other than the humans is there. A hissing noise is heard constantly, and from the towers a cloud of purple steam rises from the ground and quickly diffuses in the air. Some of that stuff has drifted up here, bringing a taste of rotten eggs.

Be patient, boy; catch a breath first before pushing your shoulders through. You know, that emu is in a cage in the zoo. Plonk took me to see the poor soul. They still feed the bird with bread soaked in booze. The canvas hat and bloody red tie.

Muru points his snout toward the plant and howls. I doubt if the dog is complaining about the rotten-egg smell; the hissing is

212

what worries him. The noise sounds like a serpent. Indeed, there might be one there; a monstrous one wallowing in the dust of the crushed rocks, and if it crawls out, the beast could snatch us all up. That happened to the Wawalags.

Up on the Mount Wawalag slopes, two oval stones clap and the call "Bugalili, Bugalili . . ." echoes from the sky. Hear that, Urban? The wise old man is calling you. He'll make you into *marngit*. When you're a medicine man, you'll carry a dilly bag full of *dal* and heal the country.

Muru howls, though his call sounds sane now.

No, they will not make a *marngit* of you. No woman has ever been a medicine man.

The oval stones clap: "Bugalili . . . !" Why have the spirits changed their will? I had made that tiny spear, carried it all the way with me.

Don't cry, my boy . . . you are a girl. Be sweet; the *balandas* are not here forever. As soon as they go you'll bring life to the trees and rocks again.

At dawn I should clear away every blood stain and bury the traces so the smell doesn't drift away. That will keep off *wurulu*. Yes, I dreamed about Wuluru last night. She brought me a bundle of cotton wads and a blanket, that same one she handed to me in the enclosure in town. "Your spirit boss will opt for a girl, surely. Only a woman could make the tribe live again."

We'll make it on our own, girl, just as the Wawalags did and the tribe spread—Honeyeater, Oyster, Lizard, Owl, Cockatoo, Ant, *Ulundnwi*, Snake, Turtle. I'll tell you all about them and many, many more as soon as you grow up. Marngit will be here to talk to you in your dreams, too.